# Deadly Encounters

# An anthology

## Jeannie Wycherley

# DEDICATION

For my husband, John Wycherley, with all my
love.

*So true a fool is love, that in your will,*
*Though you do anything, he thinks no ill..*

# CONTENTS

# A CONVERSATION WITH DEATH

Another unbearably warm night. Feeling hot and sticky, in spite of flinging the windows wide before coming to bed, I felt as though I would suffocate in the stuffy air. Beside me, my husband James snored under the pile of covers, but he wasn't overheating. Something to do with my age then.

I slipped out of bed and groped blindly around for a discarded t-shirt. A wet nose gently touched my fingers, and I scratched the fuzzy brow of my beloved pooch, Charlie. He lay down again, old now, but contented enough. I would never love a creature more than I did him.

The clunk of my bamboo wind chime drifted through the windows, signifying a breeze outside. I pulled on my t-shirt and padded through the house, unlocking the patio doors, stepping out onto the decking. I felt the sweat prickle on my skin as it dried. Instant relief.

Movement at the bottom of the garden.

I scrutinized the darkness. Nothing to see. A fox? Most likely one of the neighbour's cats. I walked in bare feet across the lawn to our picnic table and chairs, relishing the slick coolness of the grass between my toes.

I was almost at the decked area when I noticed the figure sitting in my chair. The hooded black cloak made for wonderful camouflage in the dark. I started in alarm, my heart beating hard in my chest, but the figure raised a hand, not in friendship but as a signal for me to pause. I caught my breath. Waited. A pale finger indicated the chair next to it. My eyes flicked towards the house. Should I make a run for it?

"Sit." The voice of a woman. Assured. Calm. I sat.

"Who are you?" I asked, casting a longing look back over my shoulder at my open bedroom windows. Perhaps my husband would wake up.

"I am death," the woman replied.

The air was still as I processed this. Death? My fingers twitched against the armrests of my seat, and I leaned forward to get a better look at the woman. I still couldn't see her face, just a pale countenance buried deep beneath the hood of the cloak. She was clearly staring at me though.

A lunatic, surely?

"Oh." Horror movies had taught me how imperative it was to keep the crazy killer talking until help arrived. What does one talk to Death about? "Why are you here?"

"I've come to collect," she said, her voice low and sincere, almost apologetic. It wasn't what I wanted to hear.

"Oh," I repeated, unsure of what else to say.

I swayed backwards in my seat and took a deep breath. Would James find my corpse here in the morning? Would he be devastated? I hoped so. But perhaps he would relish his freedom. I had him under false pretences in many ways.

"False pretences?"

I looked at Death in horror. Her interest was clearly piqued. But I had not articulated my thoughts aloud.

A noise that sounded a little like a giggle emanated from deep within the folds of the cloak. "Death is legion.

We are many. We know all."

"All." Of course Death would know all. I folded my hands in my lap and looked down at them. In the moonlight, I could see the faint trace of what I had assumed would one day be liver spots, but I should have had another twenty or thirty years ahead of me. Undeserved time, perhaps? This would be my day of reckoning. I had known I would have to face it eventually, and to be honest, lately, the fear of it had been eating away at my insides.

"Will it hurt?" I asked, "the moment of dying?"

"Well now. That all depends. On how you die."

I thought longingly of James again. Over the years our passion had waned, but he remained the one I always wanted, had fought to be with. I wanted to fling myself down on the grass and beat against the earth, beg for my life, spend more time with him. Appreciate him more.

"Some people die very painful deaths." The woman's contemplative voice interrupted my thoughts. Behind me somewhere, a rope creaked stiffly. I stifled a shriek. In my mind's eye I could see the dangle of a noose.

I bit back my fear, took a deep ragged breath of air and stared wildly around at the dark spaces of my garden. "Is she here too?" I whispered, my voice hollow with fear.

"Who?" asked Death.

"Cecily."

I hadn't said her name out loud in years. It escaped now. A hiss. A will of the wisp. Hushed words darting nervously around the garden. A firefly set free from the darkest recess of my memory.

"Something you need to confess?" Death goaded me.

I thought of Cecily, the way she had been when I first met her in those heady days of college. We had shared a

3

house. Me, her, and my friend Lara.

"She seemed different to us. A different background. At the time we saw her as ... a lower caste ... if you like ..." It sounded repugnant to me now.

"I don't."

"No." I could see that nobody would like it.

While we spent our money on endless supplies of cut price designer gear and nights out, Cecily wore discount store jeans and t-shirts, checked shirts and trainers, and nothing else. Because she had nothing else. Cecily could pack all of her belongings into a single medium suitcase. She had spent years in foster care because her mother had been a drug addict unable to cope with a daughter she hadn't wanted in the first place. Cecily moved from pillar to post, but she always adapted. Wherever she went, she took her books and her sunny nature with her. She studied while we partied, and we despised her for it. We treated her badly, yes we did, but she never complained. She was sweet natured and forgiving, and we took advantage of that—counted on her malleability and vulnerability.

Why? Because Cecily badly wanted friends, and so we gave her our friendship, such as it was, in ways that suited us. Mostly we insisted that she be the one to wash up and tidy up, clean the bathroom, empty the bins, pay certain bills. Low level stuff. Nothing too awful. Then Lara—finding herself up against an impending deadline for an important piece of coursework—coaxed Cecily to write a paper for her. Lara passed her module with flying colours, and after that we both demanded Cecily's 'help'. Cecily didn't like doing it—this cheating—but we insisted.

Still, Cecily remained sweet tempered and patient, just as she had always been. We took her to parties when she wanted to tag along, which wasn't often. I didn't consider her particularly attractive and so didn't see her as a rival for anyone's affections. That was my mistake.

Making a play for James was hers.

Tall, athletic, blond, and beautiful, James was my dream man. We had been dating for a few months and everything had been going well. I worked hard at keeping him interested. But then one night at a party, I brought Cecily along and realized he was making eyes at her. I went into the kitchen to pour us drinks, and when I returned, they were huddled together, sharing personal space, his eyes on her mouth, her smiling at his words.

I sidled in between them. Handed James his drink. Led him away. When he glanced back at Cecily, just that once, I knew I had to do something or lose him forever.

"He meant everything to me."

Death made a snorting noise. "Truly?"

What was Death getting at? I loved James. I did. But yes, he was from a good family, had great connections. He studied business at University and intended on joining the family firm. A bright future beckoned. I wanted to be part of that future. I had no other ambitions for myself. I intended to have some sort of career, but I didn't care what road I took. I had no intention of working myself to the bone.

But if I chose to be totally honest? I guess James was my best hope for the huge house of my dreams, along with an upstanding position in the community.

I felt Death's eyes upon me. My palms pricked with fear.

"He had to be mine. She could have ruined it all."

"What did you do?"

I had been furious. A red mist of anger descended upon me, and although I giggled and flirted with James for the rest of the evening, my mind slowly churned a dense hatred into a pernicious plan. James drank a little too much, and so being the accommodating and dutiful girlfriend that I was, I persuaded him to leave his car in my care and go off clubbing with his friends.

I roped in Lara, also the worse for wear, and explained what had happened. Being a good friend, she shared my outrage. At the end of the evening, we located Cecily who seemed uneasy. Perhaps she sensed that she had overstepped my mark with James, I don't know. We coaxed her into the car. Then when it became apparent we weren't driving home, she questioned me.

"We thought we'd have a little more fun," I said and smiled, my face nearly breaking under the duplicity of it all. Cecily settled into her seat, but her eyes were worried.

I drove us to the Devil's Stack, a local geological anomaly, and a place I knew well. I had a part time job there, selling ice cream and tourist tat. Under the dark brooding sky, while the clouds chased across the moon, we could make out the enormous boulders that nature had piled on top of each other at some point in earth's pre-history. The wind blew through the stacks making an eerie sound. Beneath them were an equally odd set of naturally occurring caves. During the day the area teemed with walkers and families having picnics. In the evening, the place remained locked up.

But not completely. I led my friends down to the entrance of Blue John, a cave known for the brilliance of the blue gems embedded within the stone. I had brought along a flashlight from James's car, and Lara had her phone. We used these to illuminate the way. Then we spent a little time supposedly goofing around, walking deeper into the cave, although Cecily's quietness and reluctance to join in was irksome, to say the least. I caught her looking at the exit numerous times.

Finally, I found what I was looking for. A small enclosed cave used to store postcards and ice cream cones. I unlocked the entrance and moved in first. Lara stepped politely back to allow Cecily through. As soon as Cecily entered the cave, I did an about turn, exited and slammed the wooden door tightly shut, sending the bolt noisily home.

Lara hooted with laughter at how easy it had all been. Cecily screamed and banged on the door. I put my face to the crack and shouted in, "Stay away from James, you bitch! He belongs to me."

"And then we left," I told Death.

"What happened to Cecily?"

I shrugged, non-committal. I chose not to think about it. Someone had found her and set her free. I never saw her again. I assumed she had not completed her degree course.

A hand shot out and icy fingers cruelly pinched my arm. I saw the scene through Death's eyes, felt Cecily's terror.

The wall of the cave felt rough against my back. Water trickled down from the ceiling, and the weight of hundreds of thousands of tons of solid rock, mere inches from my head, pressed down on me. Surely there was no air? I couldn't breathe! Claustrophobic and terrified, I moved forward to bang my fists hard against the door, but its solidity defied me. I heard myself on the other side—words that in my panic I couldn't quite catch. Laughter. Footsteps dying away.

Alone in the darkness, gasping and weeping, I knelt, searching for the gap between the floor and the door, my fingers scrabbling against the freezing cold stone. In the corner behind me, I heard something move. Shrieking, I pummelled the door harder, then dug my nails into the ground, frantically trying to make the miniscule gap wider—praying it would offer me air and an escape. Something brushed against my face, and I squealed. My bladder released, and my jeans were suddenly warm and wet. A spider. That was all.

And yet ... something kept me company, something I couldn't see. I heard it breathing. Rasping. An echo of my own tortured breaths. I could sense it moving. I lashed out blindly, wildly flailing my arms around, my clenched fists connecting with the solid walls. Over and over I struck out until my hands were a bloodied, pulpy mess. I screamed and shrieked until my throat felt scratchy and raw, and then, because the pain in my hands throbbed with intensity, I struck the door with my head. Bang. And then again. And again. And again.

"Help me. Help me." My voice, a husky whisper, kept time. I would die down here. No-one would come.

I violently ripped my arm from Death's grasp and turned away from her. "Someone came. They did."

"At nine the next morning." Yes, someone would open up. It would be a long night for Cecily, nonetheless.

"She survived! I saw it in the paper."

"You saw what exactly?"

"I saw ... I saw ..." I shrank away from what I had seen. Death stared me down.

"She thought she'd been possessed. She killed herself." My voice broke. "Not long after. She hung herself." The creaking of her rope had haunted my dreams ever since. I might as well have killed Cecily myself. I'd understood that fact for thirty years. I'd lived with the knowledge buried deep within me. "I needed to have James though. Whatever the cost."

Death remained silent.

I shuddered. "And now you've come for me."

What awaits us when we pass? How painful will death be? Would I burn in hell for all eternity?

But Death shook her head, and a familiar figure had scampered up to us. "No," Death said. "I've come for Charlie." My faithful hound wagged his tail, his eyes shining as he looked happily up at Death. "Your time will come soon enough," she said to me. "But you'll suffer on this earthly plane first." And then Death had gone, and I found myself alone, my mouth open, my heart broken, Charlie suddenly lying motionless at my feet.

"Zoe?" I slowly turned at the sound of James's voice. He had crept up behind me, and listened to my conversation with death. Now his face clouded. "Who were you talking to? What did you do to Cecily?"

# TO THE SUMMER SWEET

Standing by the battered front door, picking at red flaking paint and rotten wood with my thumbnail, I watched the quiet road for signs of life. I tried not to show my impatience as the lawyer's representative finally slithered up the drive in her slinky woollen suit. Not that she was late, quite the contrary, but I was eager to get down to business.

I watched her sidestep some tall weeds growing through the cracked slabs of the front path. She trod on a snail, pulled a disgusted face and made a low eww sound before hastily smiling at me and presenting her hand.

"Dr Crawley?" she asked in a sing-song voice, "I'm Emily Moore from Bartram, Barrett and Lowndes."

I took her hand—young, warm, and moist—and shook it with my own cool, dry grip. "Pleased to meet you," I lied. As if I cared. This woman was a means to an end, that's all. I could exchange pleasantries of course, but really I would rather not.

"Are you a medical doctor?" she asked. I rolled my eyes inwardly. Such a predictable question. "No, not as such. I have a PhD in criminology."

She drew in her breath excitedly. "Really? How interesting. I would love to have studied something like that at University. Didn't get the grades." It didn't surprise me. I nodded politely. "I love all those shows on the telly, you know, *CSI*, *NCIS*, *Silent Witness*. Any murder mysteries and I'm hooked." So mundane. I nodded again but didn't reply. A cloud passed over Emily's eyes for just a second as she scrutinised me, but she recovered quickly and flashed her smile again.

"Anyway, enough frivolity. I should take you inside. I have all the paperwork ready for you to sign." She produced a small bunch of keys from her shoulder bag. They were labelled with a parcel tag that clearly said *14 Sandilands Drive*. An address I knew well. Very well. A little thrill pulsed through me.

Emily turned her key in the main lock and gave a little push. The door was old and the weather had warped the wood so that it stuck, then gave a reluctant shudder when Emily forced it open. She stood back, politely allowing me to enter first. The house was stuffy after being shut up for so long, smelling faintly musty but not damp. All personal possessions were long gone, but the carpets, curtains and some heavier pieces of furniture were still in situ, together with wallpaper that had been on the walls for the best part of forty years, lending a quaint retro feel to the house.

"Obviously you're aware that the property hasn't been inhabited for a long time, Dr Crawley?" she asked. "I believe that your father bought it after the previous owner's relatives applied to have the estate dissolved."

"That's correct.'" I said. All my life my parents had lived next door to this property. My father had bought the house after it had stood empty for a number of years. He had harboured the intention of extending his grounds and demolishing this house, but his recent, sudden death had put paid to such plans. Now I had inherited everything, including this house.

Emily gossiped happily. "It belonged to a Mrs Summer? She disappeared about ten years ago. Her family had to have her declared dead. I heard that she ran off with her young Moroccan lover. Maybe she's still enjoying the high life somewhere."

"Could be." I smiled coldly but smirked inwardly at the idea that the stern, uptight Mary Louise Summer had ever had any lovers, let alone a handsome Moroccan one. No man in his right mind would have ventured near her.

"How very mysterious it all is." Emily giggled. "Just right for a criminologist."

"Indeed it is. Perfect," I agreed. It had actually been me that started that rumour. A young Moroccan student had worked in Mrs Summer's precious garden occasionally and tongues had wagged. Heaven knows what happened to him, but if he had returned to North Africa, it hadn't been in the company of Mrs Summer, of that I was certain.

I led Emily into the kitchen so that we could get started on the paperwork. "It will just take me a few minutes to get all this together," she said, pulling a file and an iPad from her bag.

"No problem," I said, "I'll just have a quick mosey around if you don't mind." And without waiting for an answer, I returned to the entrance hallway and headed for the stairs. I climbed into the light streaming into the hallway from the stained glass window halfway up the stairs. With every step I took, the old carpet emitted little puffs of dust that sparkled and danced in the light, like nothing in this sad house had ever done before.

I knew where I was heading. The layout of the house mirrored my parents' house. In the back bedroom, I pressed my forehead against the grimy window and peered out over the garden, smiling at the overgrowth, the brambles, bushes, and wild roses. I cast my mind back to how the garden had looked thirty years before.

I had been eight. It had been the first summer where

I'd had permission to explore farther afield than Sandilands Drive. With my friends Ian, Karen, Joe, and Jo, I had ridden my bike out into the country and down to the canal, and we had created dens, formed secret societies, sworn pacts of eternal friendship and generally had a great time. I was a happy, healthy kid. Then I had caught measles and the summer continued without me. My friends added a new member to the gang, and I was temporarily forgotten. My house and garden became my entire world.

My greatest friend at that time had been Sampson. Sampson had been a tiger. Okay, really he was a stripy cat who wasn't even orange. The stripes were like a tiger's but the resemblance ended there. Sampson was a pussycat in all the ways that mattered. Neither fierce nor ferocious; he was friendly, loving, and vocal. I adored him although he didn't belong to me. I had no idea of his real name, or even if he was a he. I just liked the name Sampson. I cherished his daily visits, and on fine days I played with him for as long as he would let me. On wet days I sat in my bedroom, opened the window and called to him. My parents didn't allow him in the house so we would look at each other mournfully through the glass, and he would meow.

Finally, slightly later than the other children, I rejoined school. I felt tired, itchy and morose that first day, yearning to hurry home to Sampson. At the bell I rushed home, ran as fast as my weak little legs would carry me, dashed past Mum in the kitchen and straight out into our garden. I called for Sampson and listened. I heard an answering meow from next door so I wandered over to the fence, searching for somewhere low enough for me to be able to see over.

Mrs Summer was our less than friendly neighbour.

Probably in her early forties at the time, she seemed far older. I don't know who or where her husband was. Mrs Summer lived alone and hated children, noise and jollity. Woe betide any child who kicked a ball into her garden. I found her quite intimidating, so I raised my head above the fence slowly and quietly.

What I saw stayed with me forever. Mrs Summer held Sampson by the scruff of his neck in one hand. In the other she held a knife. With one quick movement, she slit the cat's throat and tossed him onto her compost heap where he lay, twitching and shuddering. I bolted backwards, sick to my stomach. She turned, saw me, and sneered. She gestured at me with her knife; threatening me.

"Stay out of my garden!" she hissed. I collapsed on the ground, shaking, a combination of terror and grief. She had killed my beloved Sampson!

I ran howling into my house, destroyed by what I had witnessed. My parents understood but were dismissive; what could they do? As an adult, they considered Mrs Summer somehow untouchable. The cat had been a pest. Mrs Summer was therefore within her rights.

Remembering all this, I walked solemnly downstairs and opened the door into the garden. I squeezed my way through the undergrowth, to a dilapidated old shed and the large compost heap to the rear. Emily followed me out, making noises about what a lovely garden this could be. The sun shone down on us momentarily. I gazed at the place where Sampson had died.

Emily rested her hand against a dark, spotted stain on the wall of the shed, lifting her face to the sun. I smiled fondly at the stain. Ten years ago while researching for my PhD I had visited Mrs Summer one evening, ostensibly to ask her some questions about the anti-social behaviour of the neighbourhood youngsters. Of course she knew who I was, but we didn't refer to 'the incident' of my youth. After all, I came to her as a grown-up and a respectable academic by then.

She led me proudly through her precious garden, through the hollyhocks, lilies, and roses while we chatted. Once we arrived at the compost heap, I calmly produced a sharp knife and slit her throat much as she had done to Sampson. Her blood spurted messily against the shed wall before she crumpled at my feet, gurgling but making little noticeable fuss. I dragged her body to the compost heap and buried her deeply within it. Over the next few evenings I made numerous visits to the garden, weeding, digging, filling and feeding the compost heap with all manner of nasties. Mrs Summer had never been seen again.

"What will you do with the house, Dr Crawley?" Emily asked. "Will you keep it?"

"Oh yes," I grinned. "It brings back some lovely memories. I'm thinking of getting a cat."

# RURAL DECAY

A pastel dusk had faded into darkness, and drizzle fell. The few houses I passed were quiet, soft light glowing behind drawn curtains, smoke curling from stunted chimneys. No lanterns and pumpkins here. No trick or treaters. No sense of season. Just the closed doors and minds of the fearful inhabitants of a rural village.

An absence of youngsters, a population on the verge of dying out. Soon there will be nobody left. The trees will entangle themselves around the ruins of pretty cottages and tear the stones asunder, dragging them into the marsh.

Shuffling heavily through the leaves, I follow the path to the tiny church. A bonfire burns brightly in the corner of the graveyard. Yellow flames leap from an orange heart and hypnotize; I head for its warmth, wading through grass growing tall above the graves, the stones higgledy-piggledy and covered in lichen.

I heave the load from my shoulder, drop it into the centre of the fire. Sparks explode angrily, and for a moment the fire dies back. I wait patiently. Watch entranced. Eventually the clothes start to smoulder, followed by the hair.

I like it best when the fingers and toes curl and snap.

It's All Souls' Day tomorrow, but what use are memorials when there is no-one left to remember?

# GRETEL'S REVENGE

Hansel poked the bone through the bars of the cage. The witch moved closer and stared myopically down at what she misconstrued to be his finger. Her fetid breath stank of rank meat and sour milk. Hansel turned his face away and stopped breathing in so that he wouldn't have to smell her. He feared her but was disgusted by her too. He could not abide the stink of her.

He peered at her face. Old, so old. The lines on her skin were deep, and dirt deeply engrained in the crevices around her nose and eyes. Stringy, coarse hair framed her sallow skin. Everything about her seemed dried out and crispy. A crust had formed on her lips, dry skin, flaking away. As she spoke, she festooned the space around her with spit and old food. Food figured highly in the witch's life; she was forever hungry, and she loved to eat. She craved delicate and tender meat. Make no bones about it, she planned to eat Hansel.

The witch clasped the bone between her thumb and first finger for a moment, before releasing it and unleashing a stream of vile curses at him. He scuttled backwards into the shadowy recesses of the cage still holding the bone in front of himself.

Behind the witch, Gretel banked the flames of the fire. Light flared in the small, smoky room, illuminating Hansel and the dummy finger held tightly in his hand. Gretel half expected their deception to be discovered, but light or no light, the witch was virtually blind. Cataracts clouded her yellow eyes, and she could only make out shapes and shadows.

"Tiresome child!" she shrieked and flakes of skin, repulsive snowflakes, fluttered onto her chest. "Why do you put no meat on your bones?" She slammed her hands against the bars of the cage so that it rattled. Hansel shrank back. "I'm hungry! Damn you to hell and back!"

The witch whirled about, her black skirts flaring as she did so, kicking up the dust and straw that littered the floor. "You!" she screamed at Gretel. "Build the fire under the oven. Make it hot, hot as you can. I will not starve myself for even one more night, not on your wretched brother's account. I grow weary of waiting!"

"But surely—" Gretel wanted to argue that Hansel would soon put on weight, but the witch rounded on her swiftly, striking her with a flat hand. Once, twice, three times she slapped Gretel, who twisted away and fell to the floor, her hands over her head, protecting herself.

"You have nothing to say!" The witch instructed, her voice shrill, cutting through the air. An owl roosting high in the eaves of the thatch of the cottage fluttered uneasily and turned its head away, hiding its eyes. "You miss, are meaningless. Your existence is void. Mark what I say, or I will mark you. Build the fire!" The witch kicked Gretel and swung back to Hansel. She peered into the gloom of the cage towards where she assumed Hansel shivered with fear, pulling her lips back from her teeth. Her front teeth were like tombstones, strong but black and green as though covered in moss and lichen. She hissed at Hansel, and again he turned his head from her dead stench.

Tiring of the children, she clumped noisily out of the cottage and slammed the door so hard that the owl in the eaves fluttered and feathers and dust from his wings spiralled to the floor.

Hansel moved impatiently towards the front of the cage. "Gretel!" he whispered loudly. "Gretel!"

The girl on the floor slowly uncoiled herself and sat up. Tears glistened in her eyes, but she blinked them back.

"Are you hurt?"

"No," Gretel replied. "Not really. It will pass." She stretched her arms and rolled her shoulders and took a few deep breaths. Hansel watched his sister with concern.

"We have to get out of here. You have to find a way to release me from this cage."

"I don't know what to do!" Gretel rubbed her dirty face with even dirtier hands. "You know she carries the key on the chain around her waist. I can't steal it from her. Even when she sleeps she has one eye open."

"There must be another way."

From outside, deep in the forest, they heard a lone wolf howling, a chilling sound. Gretel shuddered. She went to the door and opened it a tiny crack, peering out. Her breath steamed when she breathed.

"It's cold out there. There'll be a deep frost in the morning." She sighed and closed the door, turned her attention back to the fire. She would build it, and it would warm the occupants of this evil cottage, but then the witch would come back and ... Gretel looked at her brother. It didn't bear thinking about. The witch would burn him alive and then eat him. Unless ...

\*\*\*

The witch returned much later, carrying herbs that she had collected in the forest. She was now starving and even more foul-tempered. She glared at both children.

19

"I will hang the cauldron, and you can start heating the water, girl," she instructed, and Gretel hurried to do her bidding. The cauldron was large and extremely heavy. It hung from a large iron hook in the alcove above the oven, and Gretel could not lift it, yet the witch could heft it easily with one hand. She had amazing strength.

Gretel had to climb onto a stool in order to be able to reach high enough to pour water from a bucket into the cauldron. The cauldron held eight buckets of water, and Gretel drew each bucket from the well. Filling the cauldron was a slow and tiresome business, and all the time that Gretel laboured, the oven grew hotter and hotter.

By the time the cauldron had been filled, the witch had finished kneading some dough that she had prepared earlier in the day.

"We will bake first," she said. The witch liked nothing better than a thick nutritious boy stew flavoured with fresh herbs, accompanied by freshly baked bread.

"Girl!" The witch smiled slyly at Gretel. "We need to ensure the oven is the correct temperature." She looked towards the oven with her yellow eyes. Flames darted out from the sides of the oven. "Creep in," said the witch. "See if it is properly heated. Then I will know that I can bake my bread to perfection."

Gretel stared at the oven, now so hot that the door glowed red and orange. She observed as the flames flicked at the sides and understood that once she put her head into the oven, the witch would push her in and shut the door. The witch had obviously grown tired of both of the children. She intended to eat Gretel too. Gretel might have been young, but she wasn't stupid, and she had a plan.

"Oh gracious witch," she cried. "I cannot see how I

can possibly do as you ask. How do I get in?" She fell to her knees in supplication. "Please do not be angry with me. I only wish to attend you!"

"Foolish child!" hissed the witch, her eyes burning with annoyance. "The door is plenty big enough to allow you access!"

"No ma'am!" cried Gretel plaintively. "I fear it is not!"

"Silly goose," spat the witch. "That oven door is enormous. Just look, I can climb in myself." She walked purposely towards the oven and flung open the door with her bare hand. Leaning down, she thrust her head into the oven.

Gretel acted quickly. Leaping to her feet, she drove both hands into the witch's ample rump. She pushed hard against the witch's buttocks with all of her strength and drove the old woman hard into the oven. The witch yelled and shrieked in raw agony. Gretel had no doubt that her blood curdling screams would be heard all over the forest. She slammed the door shut and fastened the bolt. The witch was trapped.

The shrieking continued but only for a short while. To Gretel and Hansel, the witch's screams were music to their ears. A lullaby of freedom.

The oven roared and burned, and Gretel attended to it for a while. The stench of burning flesh seemed overpowering at times, but Gretel bore it because Hansel remained trapped in his cage and he had no choice but to inhale the fetid, fatty stink. Towards dawn, the fire began to die down, and Gretel left it. She slept on the floor beside Hansel's cage for a few hours while Hansel watched over her, keeping one eye firmly on the locked door of the oven.

When Gretel awoke, she lay for a moment on the hard floor, testing her body for aches and pains. Sitting, she remembered the events of the night before and immediately hurried to open the door of the oven to peer in. Smiling at Hansel, she rushed out of the cottage and drew a bucket of fresh water from the well. She re-entered the cottage and doused the burning embers of the oven.

Picking up a large wooden spoon, generally used to stir the contents of the huge cauldron, Gretel poked her head into the rapidly cooling oven and scraped the remains of the fire out onto the floor around her feet. Once she had managed to scrape out the bulk of the ash and detritus, she squatted on her haunches and sifted through the mess with her fingers.

She searched among fragments of charred wood, pieces of material, slivers of bone and unidentifiable chunks of matter that were congealed, foul-smelling and smoking. Finally, she found it—the key to Hansel's cage. Gretel picked it up, burning her fingers, and quickly threw it into the bucket. She washed it thoroughly in what remained of the water, wiping it free of the gruesome gore and burnt flesh that clung to it. When it was clean, she stood stiffly and stepped over the mess on the floor to unlock the cage and set Hansel free.

"We did it!" breathed Hansel. "We can go home." Gretel laughed and embraced her brother and arm in arm they walked towards the cottage door. Hansel stood on the threshold and breathed in the fresh cold air of the frosty day outside, but Gretel turned back. Reaching back into the heap of burnt offerings on the floor she extracted a bone.

It was a small bone. It had once been part of the witch's right hand, probably a proximal or intermediate phalange, but Gretel didn't care about this. She trusted the urge she felt, something inside her that nagged her to take it away. It would come in useful later.

She joined Hansel at the cottage door, and together they stepped out into the cold day and started on the long journey through the forest in search of the home they had been forced to leave just four weeks previously. Every step of the way, Gretel thought about the circumstances that had led to their encounter with the witch; the way her stepmother had managed to persuade their father that he would be better off without his children. She considered how weak-willed her father had been, but she chose to forgive him because she loved him. She recognized that deep inside he sincerely loved his children even though he had a genuine fear of his second wife.

A grudge began to burn brightly in Gretel's heart. All the way home she kept a tight hold of the bone in her pocket. She began to plot against her stepmother. The time had arrived to take revenge.

\*\*\*

The children's homecoming was jubilant. The woodcutter, overjoyed to be reunited with his beloved Hansel and Gretel, cried genuine tears and embraced them over and over, swearing he would never, ever let them go again. The children clung to him. Hansel wept, overcome with emotion, but Gretel remained guarded, ever wary and watchful.

The stepmother stood beside him, her smile stiff and forced. Her teeth were gritted in a grimace that could possibly pass for a grin, but her eyes were cold and her stomach churned with the knowledge that her plan had been thwarted. Her heart beat hard against her chest and she wondered whether there would be any repercussions for her actions in forcing the woodcutter to abandon the children in the forest. She wondered what her neighbours were saying, but she lifted her chin and pretended to be as happy as her fool of a husband.

To fend off unwanted criticism, the stepmother threw a lavish party and organized a feast to welcome the children home. It really wasn't in the stepmother's nature to do any work, so she simply organized the neighbours to fetch their tables and best linen and to each contribute food and drink to the gathering. The whole village turned out for the festivities and merriment ensued, with singing and dancing and drunken revelry aplenty. Children raced around playing tag, and hide and seek, long into the night. Behind Farmer Grimm's barn, couples carelessly rolled in the hay and whispered endearments, men made oaths, and women broke theirs. A good time was had by all.

Hansel stood on a table among a great crowd of people, telling and retelling his story. He added embellishments to make it sound even more dramatic than it had actually been and in several notable tellings, he placed Gretel in the cage while he became her saviour and disposed deftly of the witch himself.

Through it all Gretel remained stern-faced and focused. She kept close to her stepmother, smiling sweetly whenever anyone looked her way or addressed her. Secretly, she observed the stepmother's every move and bided her time. When the stepmother's pewter goblet was empty, Gretel would rush to refill it for her. Time and again she filled the vessel with the hardest liquor she could find.

"Why Gretel," purred the stepmother, "you have become such an attentive and kind stepdaughter since your, ah, adventure in the forest."

Gretel nodded seriously. "I have realized that having such wonderful family and friends is a true blessing, dearest Mother."

"Indeed it is," slurred the stepmother in response.

"I intend to protect that blessing to the best of my ability," Gretel murmured. "Here, Mother, take some more of this." With a flourish, and before the stepmother could argue, Gretel refilled the goblet and handed it back to her. "Drink to our good health, Mother! Our continued good health!"

All around them, friends and neighbours took up the cry, "Good health! Good health!" And so the stepmother drank deeply. It wasn't long before she slumped on her stool, her eyes glassy and her mouth a dribbling O.

\*\*\*

There were several sore heads the next morning, of which the most severe belonged to none other than the stepmother. She lay in bed clutching her forehead and moaning; periodically she turned her head and vomited into a bucket that Gretel had thoughtfully provided for her.

"Oh, I feel terrible," moaned the stepmother. Gretel sat beside her and gently mopped her face and brow with a cool, clean cloth. "I fancy I have a deadly affliction. I am ready to meet my maker." The fumes she gave off quite reminded Gretel of the wicked witch's stinking breath. Gretel heartily wished the stepmother would join her maker. Soon.

"I am so sorry for that," soothed Gretel.

"It is your fault, you wicked, wicked girl," scolded the stepmother. "If it hadn't been for you, I would never have partaken of so much liquor, and I wouldn't feel this way."

Gretel hung her head in shame. "You are correct,

Mother. I am quite at fault and I throw myself on your mercy. How can I possibly ever make it up to you?"

The stepmother turned abruptly on her side and vomited again, purposefully missing the bucket beside the bed. She grimaced and threw herself back on the pillows.

Gretel mopped her face again.

"Have no fear, Mother. I will clean your room and change your bed and make everything smell fresh and clean. I will make up for my misdeeds to you in a million different ways." She stood up and turned to go but stopped and placed her hand on her stepmother's forehead. "In fact, I shall make you a glorious healing chicken stew. It is perfect for over-indulgence."

"That does sound good," the stepmother mumbled weakly.

"Oh it is. I promise I'll have you feeling better in no time." Gretel smiled and headed for the kitchen.

In the four weeks or so that Hansel and Gretel had spent with the wicked witch deep in the forest, Gretel had learned a number of new skills. Creating soups and stews in the witch's cauldron had been one of those. The witch had also issued instructions for Gretel in the picking and cleansing of herbs from the forest. Now, armed with all of this new knowledge, Gretel set about creating the most delicious stew.

She took the biggest iron pan she could find and fried onion in a little butter before adding sage and salt. Quickly she added chicken skin and diced carrots and fried them for a while. From there she added a little water and more vegetables and cubes of chicken. Once everything had softened slightly, Gretel added more water and brought it to a boil. She tempered the heat before adding herbs that she had collected bright and early that morning as the sun danced through the trees on the edge of the forest.

Into the stew went finely chopped angelica, avens, and asafoetida, herbs to purify and protect. Bay and buckthorn, mastic and carnation followed—before Gretel finally added a huge amount of turnip to bring about the end of a relationship, along with a handful of wormwood, needed if she were to call a spirit. Gretel knew that the combination of herbs would remain largely innocuous without the final ingredient. Once the stew had been brought once more to boiling point, she slipped the small bone from the witch's house into the pot, and then she stirred and stirred the mixture with a long wooden ladle.

The mixture bubbled and grew darker and darker, and the steam rising from the pot appeared greenish-grey. The kitchen filled with the stink of soiled laundry and rancid cesspits. Gretel gagged, and her eyes watered, but still she stirred, focussing all the time on the mixture in the cooking pot.

After some time, the grim colour of the stew faded and the mixture began to resemble a chunky chicken stew once more. Gretel nodded with satisfaction, placed a lid on the pot and left the kitchen in order to set about undertaking various other chores for her stepmother. Hansel looked on curiously, watching his sister clean the stepmother's bedroom, change her sheets, bathe her, and fetch and carry as per the stepmother's every wish.

The tempting aroma of chicken stew filled the woodcutter's little house. The stepmother lifted her nose and sniffed appreciatively, before plaintively asking Gretel how much longer her supper would be. Gretel smiled. "I'll bring you some straight away Mother, if you think your stomach can stand it?"

"I can try a little, can't I?" murmured the stepmother weakly. Gretel nodded and went through to the kitchen.

She rummaged around for the largest bowl she could find, and then, taking a ladle, she filled the bowl to the brim and returned to the stepmother's bedside.

The stepmother observed the stew, then made a greedy grab for the tray. Without further ado, she started ladling the stew straight into her mouth, barely pausing to chew the chunks. Within a few minutes the stepmother had emptied the bowl, and was looking expectantly at Gretel.

Gretel refilled the bowl. Once again, the stepmother polished off the whole lot in a short space of time.

This time the stepmother slumped back against the pillows of her freshly changed bed, looking slightly red in the face.

"Are you quite well, Mother?" asked Gretel sweetly.

"Perfectly!" snapped the stepmother, and Gretel bowed her head.

"In that case, I really ought to serve the rest of the stew to Hansel. He has not eaten all day."

The stepmother thought about this for a moment. She really didn't appreciate the idea of Hansel finishing off the stew. It would be such a waste to give that wretched boy decent food. He could make do with the leftovers from the previous night's party. If there were any. If there weren't, he could always have bread and jam.

"No, no!" She sat up abruptly. "I, er, I think it's useful in medicinal terms. Perhaps I should have one more bowl. Just one more."

This pleased Gretel. Enough stew remained for one more bowl and then the stepmother would have consumed everything. She carefully drained the remains of the pot into the bowl and scraped out everything before returning to the stepmother's bedroom and handing it over.

This time the stepmother ate more slowly. Although full to bursting, she was determined not to leave a single drop. Swallowing the very last morsel, the stepmother suddenly stopped and made a small noise in her throat.

"Mother?" enquired Gretel. "Is everything all right?"

The stepmother coughed. Then she tried to clear her throat.

"I've swallowed a bone," she forced out. Then she started coughing again.

Gretel pulled the stepmother farther upright and made a great show of slapping her back as though to dislodge the bone. It wouldn't shift. Gretel thumped the stepmother hard between the shoulder blades. The stepmother cried out, and Gretel did it again with great relish.

Nothing appeared to help. The stepmother coughed and hacked, hacked and coughed. Time and again she tried to clear her throat but nothing would move it. The bone remained lodged squarely in the stepmother's throat. The stepmother stuck her own fingers down her throat in an effort to retrieve it, resulting in her regurgitating the stew all over her clean bed.

Gretel let her lay in the mess.

They sent for a doctor, and he pronounced the situation grave. He made an attempt, with small pliers, to prise the bone from its home, but only succeeded in pushing the bone farther into the throat where it could not be reached by any of his instruments.

The stepmother collapsed back on her bed wheezing and coughing. Her face tinged with red from the effort of breathing. Her throat was sore from all of the attempted interventions and the repeated hacking cough.

Gretel hovered by the stepmother's side, looking for all the world like a loving and concerned daughter, but inside her soul sang.

***

That night Gretel offered to sit with the stepmother as she dozed fitfully between bouts of restlessness and laboured breathing. Her throat seemed to be swelling, and the flesh on her face was puffy and pink. Her eyes were tiny slits. Gretel looked on in wonder.

Dawn brought a change. The stepmother's eyes suddenly flew open. She clutched at her throat and opened her mouth. To Gretel, sitting just a few feet away from her on her hard stool, it appeared as though the stepmother was trying to scream but was unable to make any noise.

The stepmother clawed at her throat with both hands, her eyes wide open in shock. She looked beseechingly at Gretel and then threw her head forward as though she were about to vomit again. Her back bucked, and her torso shuddered. Once, twice, three times she retched. Saliva dripped down her chin. Then she straightened up again, and at last Gretel could see the effects that her special chicken stew had produced on the stepmother.

The stepmother's mouth gaped but her eyes were tightly closed. Two fingers poked out of her mouth, seeking freedom. The two fingers were joined by a third and then a fourth.

The nails were long but broken, ragged and filthy. Dirt had embedded itself deeply around the cuticles. The fingers themselves were mottled a light shade of green and yet oddly dry. Gretel could see the skin flaking where they rubbed against the stepmother's lips.

The fingers curled around the lower lip, trying to find purchase, slipping and scratching as they gripped at the spittle flecked chin. The stepmother's cheeks pulsed. The mouth was being forced open, impossibly wide. Slight splits appeared in the corners of the mouth and blood bloomed against the pale skin. Somewhere in the stepmother's mouth, the thumb and the rest of the hand were trying to find room to get themselves out. With a pop and a crack, the stepmother's lower jaw detached itself from the upper jaw, and the hand and its wrist slid from the stepmother's mouth, landing on her stomach with a soft plop. Gretel clapped a hand to her mouth to stop herself from screaming and alerting the rest of the household. She instinctively pushed her stool backwards in repulsion.

The stepmother's eyes opened. Her hands went straight to her ruined jaw and she moaned; a deep despairing sound. She cradled her jaw, completely ignoring the hand that twitched and flexed against her stomach.

Revolted, Gretel shrank against the wall, unable to take her eyes from the hand. The ragged edges of the flesh at the wrist pulsated with renewed life. The pink-grey veins that had dragged limply behind the hand as it dropped from the stepmother's mouth lengthened and turned a deeper red. Gretel saw flesh growing around the wound. The wrist morphed, becoming an arm. A terrified Gretel shivered. What had she unleashed?

The fingers lifted, scenting their prey. The hand flopped back on itself and started to crawl up the stepmother's stomach, onto her chest and up to her neck. The mottled hand twisted itself so that the thumb sat just underneath the stepmother's jawline with the fingers stretched out on the other side.

And then the hand started to squeeze.

The hand had great strength. Gretel remembered how

strong the witch had been, and she wasn't the least surprised. Of course the hand would be able to throttle the stepmother all by itself. The fingers dug into the pudgy, pale flesh, while the long nails left prick marks on the tender skin. The hand tightened its grip, harder and harder, and the stepmother fell back against the pillow. Her face turned from a flaccid cream colour, to pink, to red, to a beetroot purple. Her body thrashed against the mattress for a short while. Her lips were swollen and her mouth open. Soon her tongue peeked out between the purple lips and the eyes stared up at the ceiling not seeing anything except perhaps her own mortality. Her chest bucked, once, twice and then she stopped moving altogether.

Still the hand held the stepmother by the neck. Its grip was unrelenting. It twisted the neck, this way and that, until a sharp cracking noise told Gretel that the neck had broken. The hand shook the body so that the head flopped around, much like the neck of a rag doll.

Gretel looked on while the hand—now more of a lower arm—marched down the body and grabbed the stepmother by the ankle. It made short work of dragging the body to the door. Gretel followed it, her knees quaking. It headed out of the room and towards the front door of the woodcutter's cottage. She stepped ahead of it when it paused, to open the door for it. The lower arm pulled its prize towards the forest. Gretel leaned against the door frame, watching the body disappear into the treeline to be swallowed up by the dark.

A few moments later, Gretel heard a shrieking, high-pitched laugh that chilled her blood. It sounded just like the witch. Had she now somehow completely regenerated? What would she do with the stepmother's body? Shuddering, Gretel shut the door and secured it.

There were answers that she did not want to know; questions she did not want to ask.

Not if she wanted to live happily ever after, at any rate.

# AN ENCOUNTER WITH OLD DUIR

"I wonder why that tree has kept its leaves when all the others haven't." Jane stared out of the window at the copse of trees atop a hill in the middle distance. Since they'd moved into the house in late August, Jane had delighted in the view out over the valley below, even more so when presented with evidence of the changing season. The trees had burst into brilliant colours of fire and earth, but now after a couple of stormy nights, most were bereft of foliage, with the notable exception of one huge overreaching specimen in the centre of the cluster. "Alex?" Jane prompted her husband. He grunted, barely looking up from his phone.

"It's probably an evergreen. Something Alpine," he said, returning his attention to the screen in front of him.

"Maybe." Jane didn't think this was the case. The tree appeared tall and round and full. It looked more like a large oak or beech tree, but at this distance she couldn't really tell. Curiosity would kill her for sure. "We ought to go and investigate. What do you think? Go for a walk and see if we can get up there?" Jane felt stir crazy after being cooped up over the holidays. She wanted to get out into the fresh air.

Alex glanced up again, irritated. "Mmm?" he asked, and Jane decided not to pursue the conversation any further. She quietly exited the room, and a little later she left the house, alone, car keys in hand, intent on her mission to locate the tree if she could.

She had a vague idea of how to locate the hill. It involved navigating numerous narrow back lanes that led down to the valley, then fording the river at the bottom, before making her way up the other side. Fortunately, with the exception of an enormous milk lorry and a few tractors, she encountered little traffic. Once she had a good vantage point of the top of the hill, she pulled up in a small muddy layby and took her bearings. Behind her, the coastal town where she lived splayed out, tumbling down the hill to the sea, her housing estate neatly lodged into the hillside.

There were far fewer dwellings this side of the valley; the occasional mansion or palatial bungalow, set well back from the lanes. The area was densely wooded in places, but the crest of the hill with the copse towered above everything. Jane studied the landscape; she could make out the flash of green. She was in the right vicinity.

She drove until she could progress no farther, then abandoned the car, pulling it off road and tucking it into the hedge, hoping it wouldn't cause inconvenience to anyone else.

The trees here were widely spaced, mainly silver birch and ash, with the occasional large beech. Jane pulled her walking boots on and zipped her jacket up, savouring the smell of damp earth and must. The sky above, the colour of spoiled milk, promised that the remainder of the day would only grow colder, and provided a stark relief for the skeletal branches dancing on a frigid breeze.

Jane tramped through the deep carpet of leaves, relishing kicking them with each step. The leaves were crisp, freshly fallen, in various shades of crimson, orange, and yellow. Underneath these, older leaves mouldered and decayed, scenting the woodland with a subtle and natural putrescence.

The climb to the crest of the hill was steeper than Jane had imagined. About halfway, she rested, noticing how the trees were now packed more densely than they had been lower down the hill. The trunks of the beech trees here were covered in spongey moss, and the branches above her head entwined, tapping against each other nervously.

Jane started off again, hauling herself up the last hundred yards with some difficulty. The trees congregated thickly, and brambles tore at her clothes and hair. The vicious undergrowth caused a problem. Tree roots stuck out of the earth at abrupt angles, ensuring the going was slow and treacherous. Several times Jane sucked her breath in when a thorn sliced into her naked hands, and once she slipped and wrenched her ankle. She almost considered giving the whole stupid venture up, until finally, the vegetation thinned out, and she found herself standing under the canopy of an enormous oak tree.

Jane marvelled at the sight before her. The oak's great knotted trunk must have been twenty feet in diameter at least. The lowest branches hung six feet above her head, the copious foliage a luscious, verdant green. Jane inhaled the fresh, healthy scent, feeling it tingle in her nose, and felt suddenly compelled to place her hands on the gnarled surface and run her fingers through the deep grooves. As her hands connected with the rough bark, the tree gave a distinct hum, powered by its own vibrant internal electricity.

From the other side of the trunk came a shushing noise. Someone had suddenly kicked up a pile of dry leaves. Startled, Jane pulled away from the tree, and watched as a woman walked into view.

"You made me jump!" Jane gasped, but not wanting to

appear rude she pulled herself together and smiled.

The woman gawped back at her, her mouth a toothless cavern, dark and hot. She was old. Very old. The creases carved into her face were as deep as the wrinkles in the bark of the tree, and the green of her long dress exactly matched the colour of the oak's leaves. Silver hair flowed down her back, rippling in the muted light. In spite of the freezing cold air out here, she had no shoes on.

"Greetings to you, my dear. You've come to meet Old Duir, have you?"

"Dew-ra?"

"Duir. He's mighty pleased to meet you, aren't you, old man?" The woman wheezed out a laugh and patted the tree.

Jane was perplexed. The woman had a name for the tree? Figuring discretion was the better part of valour in this case, given that the woman was obviously unsound, Jane decided to extricate herself from the situation as quickly as she courteously could.

"I'm surprised this tree has all its leaves this far into winter," she said, and began to step away.

"Duir never loses his leaves, pet."

Ridiculous. "How is that possible?" Jane frowned.

The woman looked seriously at Jane. "Well, see, like all trees, Duir keeps his leaves when he is able to draw the energy he needs from the earth. And the earth is good hereabouts, so Duir is blessed."

Jane had always assumed trees absorbed energy from light, using chlorophyll or something. She racked her brain, thinking back to school and her biology classes, but couldn't remember quite how it all worked. Perhaps the woman was right and the tree absorbed extra nutrients from the ground, but that didn't account for the fact that the leaves had remained on the tree far longer than would be considered normal.

"I keep the earth well fertilized especially for Duir, and then he sees to the rest of his needs himself."

Jane examined the ground around them. The area had been swept free of fallen leaves, and the soil had been exposed. It had not been turned over, but it appeared strangely dark and oddly rich looking.

"How?" asked Jane, unsure whether she wished to continue this conversation. Something touched the back of her neck, and irritated, she swatted it away. A moth or spider perhaps.

The woman smiled again but now she said nothing, distracted by something behind Jane, unnerving the younger woman completely. The touch came again, and Jane lifted her hand to ward off the insect but recoiled when she connected with something hard and cool. She ducked, but the thing twisted itself around her neck. Jane shouted in alarm and squirmed in its grasp, but the more she struggled, the tighter it held her. She only stopped wriggling once her feet left the ground. She found herself hoisted into the air in a hangman's grip.

With horror, Jane realized she was being held captive by a branch. The tree swung her effortlessly around itself. In a flash, she took in a man lying crumpled against Duir's enormous roots, splayed out and dead for some time by the look of it, while another female was sprawled against the trunk, her face devoid of colour, her neck at an awkward angle, but still making small movements with her mouth, seeming still alive. Just.

The branch dropped Jane next to the woman. She fell heavily, and pain flared in her knee, bright and orange. Nonetheless, she tried to scramble to her feet, rending the silence of the forest with her terrified screams. The tree was faster though. A branch shot down from above her head, sharp as an arrow, entering her right shoulder, ripping through her lung, before exiting her right buttock, impaling her against the ground.

The shock was intense, abruptly silencing Jane, who shuddered and twitched, aware that the agony had not yet fully formed but certainly would. She breathed shallowly, praying for release.

The old woman scampered like a child, delightedly clapping her hands. "Clever Duir! Clever, clever Duir!" she sang.

The tree bowed towards the women, branches waving softly, the foliage caressing Jane's cheek. She watched the veins in the leaves. They pulled away from the membrane, attracted to her skin—as leeches are drawn towards warmth. Duir began to draw Jane's life blood from her, with the lightest of touches, and Jane she finally understood the source of the nutrients he used to retain his energy and bounteous greenery. And as the light faded from Jane's reality, she focused only on her heartbeat, pulsing in time with Old Duir's humming energy and the percussive orchestration of the natural world.

# SINK OR SWIM

Sitting on the rocky shoreline, I watched as bubbles burst on the surface of the deep water, not twenty feet from me. I smiled into the salty breeze, dropping my shoulders, relaxing my neck. My skin prickled as it air-dried.

The sky shimmered, a glorious cloudless blue. Perfect for a day at the beach.

He had told me he was a merman. Did he seriously imagine I'd been born yesterday?

"Prove it," I'd said and invited him in for a swim. The anchor had just been there. I'd hooked it to his trunks.

The truth will out, one way or another.

# DOG EARED

I trod lightly, slipping up the rain-soaked alley towards the main road, clutching my trophy in a little leather pouch in my left hand. I ignored the whimpering and rustling from the dumpster behind me. The noise faded the further I moved away anyhow. I headed instead towards the sound of sanity. The shoosh of tyres on the damp streets; music drifting out of jazz bars; young men calling to short skirted, barelegged whores. I moved easily among these people of the night. They recognised me for what I was: self-contained, self-aware, unafraid, malevolent.

Home was a few short blocks away. I climbed the rambling staircase to my apartment and let myself in. It smelt clean after the streets.

Removing my boots, I stowed them neatly away before moving into the bathroom. I had redecorated this myself. I loved this pristine space. A deep, white enamel bath with stainless steel taps that glittered in the light; white marble tiles on the floor threaded with blue and bright white panelling around the lower half of the walls. The mirrors were polished until the light refracted from them like diamonds. My idea of domestic bliss.

I pulled open one part of the panelling, exposing a small cupboard, and shook two pairs of dogs' ears from my leather pouch, positioning them gently in a porcelain bowl. I covered them in salt and disinfectant, a curing bath, and left them to sit—like good little doggies. Perfect.

I stripped and showered, enjoying the feeling of being cleansed. After a night on the town I liked to pamper myself with expensive products. I liked to smell good. I inspected my clothes carefully and cleaned what may have been a patch of blood on my leather jacket. My jeans were spattered with mud, blood, and rubbish so I stowed them away with the rest of the laundry.

Finally, I could relax. I slumped on my sofa and put my feet up with a glass of good Pinot Noir. I gently caressed the nap of the leather on the sofa and reflected on a good night's work. It was late, and I was tired. I finished the wine, and my head rolled back.

I dozed.

*In my dream... was it a dream? Was it a buried memory? I see a small boy. Too old for a diaper but wearing one anyway, along with a soiled t-shirt and a dirty face. The boy smells bad. He is uncomfortable. He is standing at the end of a long dank hallway. The sun is setting and throws long shadows through the dust hovering in the stagnant air. At the far end of the hallway is the living room. The woman he calls mother sits on the sofa. He walks towards her slowly, calling for her. She pays no mind. She pets a pair of cocker spaniels. They fight to be the centre of attention, pushing their way onto her lap and licking her face. She laughs delightedly and feeds them titbits. The boy stands next to her now, reaching out to touch her arm, wanting the contact, needing the attention. She turns towards him, her heavily painted face snarling at the interruption.*

*The dogs protect her. They leap towards him, snapping and growling, their ears whipping at his face. He opens his mouth to scream.*

I sat up with a start. My heart beating hard in my chest. I had to shake off the remnants of the dream.

Nearly 3 a.m., and I needed to get some proper sleep in order to be fit for work the following morning. I stretched, moving forwards on the sofa, and suddenly heard a scratching at the front door. How peculiar. The sound of a dog asking to go out. Nails on wood, gentle scratching.

Frowning in annoyance, I moved out into the hallway and flicked the light switch. Not working. In the dim light spilling out from the living room, I could see there were no dogs at the door.

Just as well for them.

Turning away, I halted when I heard a rustling noise coming from the store cupboard. For Pete's sake! Sighing in exasperation, I moved through the dimly lit hall and grasped the cupboard handle. The noise stopped. Holding my breath, I listened closely.

Nothing.

But as soon as I dropped my hand, the rustling began again. I clasped the door handle firmly and started to turn it, but even as I did so the door was pushed open by a force inside and a large bird whipped at my face. The wings fluttered furiously, beating frantically, and dust flew around me. Choking on feathers, I tried to rip the bird away from my face, but as abruptly as it had arrived, it had gone again. I stood alone in the hallway, shaking with exertion.

Just a solitary white feather on my black t-shirt.

Okay, this seemed odd, but I couldn't let it worry me. I had too much to do. Busy, busy, busy. Over the next few days a major work project kept me occupied until late every evening. I didn't even have time to get out on to the streets and work on my trophy collection. Occasionally on my way to and from work I would catch sight of a stray dog and I would feel my bile rise. I would watch contemptuously. It scrabbled around the bins looking for food, or darted in and out of the traffic, and then conversely I would gaze longingly at it when it skipped away from me, heading off to do whatever stray dogs do during the day.

The thing about stray dogs is that they are always hungry. They may not trust you of course, not enough to come to you at first, but eventually when they are hungry enough, they will. Dogs are stupid. They're loyal. If you make friends with one you can never get rid of the damn thing. I'm not a friendly kind of guy. Not where dogs are concerned anyway. But even I can get a dog to come to me eventually. And then of course when they do, well it's a case of 'so long Fido'.

Okay, I don't know whether they all die. Maybe they don't. But there's a lot of dogs in this city that are minus their ears. I reckon it helps with their hearing if they don't have those great hairy flaps covering their ear holes. Possibly I'm doing them a favour. Who knows? And who cares? Lately, there's been some media coverage about dead dogs in dumpsters mutilated by a madman, but no-one is actually doing that much about it. Too many stray dogs for anyone to bother with.

It had been an exhausting week, so my spirits lifted when Friday rolled around. I pottered in my kitchen, produced a lasagne and a magnificent fruit salad. I cleaned up and disinfected the worktops, set the dishwasher going and then I popped a film in the DVD player and lay stomach-down on the sofa, just chilling.

*The Matrix*—a great twentieth century classic. While I certainly admired Keanu's styling, I would have preferred to live in the world the agents inhabited; sterile, no nonsense. At about the point that Neo started to learn to fight, my stomach began to itch. I scratched at it absentmindedly for a while. Five minutes later I started to scratch myself raw. I stood up and went into the bathroom and examined myself in a mirror. Small red spots covered my stomach. I had scratched the heads off a few of them and they were bleeding or weeping. I hurriedly threw off my clothes and looked myself over. The spots weren't mosquito bite sized. I wondered about measles or some strange disease. The rash appeared localized to my stomach. I hurriedly fired up my laptop and sat down naked on the sofa. I searched for photos of a red rash. Not measles. Wait. There! Flea bites. Flea bites?

I slowly looked down at the sofa. I don't have pets. I have never had pets. I don't like cats. I abhor dogs. There could be no possibility that I had fleas in the carpet, after all I had replaced every carpet in the apartment myself. That left only one possibility. The sofa.

I stood and examined it from a distance. How I loved the sofa. What a work of art. It had been designed to last me a lifetime. I had started creating it when I first moved into the apartment four years ago. I had taken an ordinary sofa, fairly expensive and very well made, and I had covered it myself. The covers had taken hours and hours of painstaking work. I had foraged, made countless trips onto the backstreets of the city under cover of the night. I bribed the neighbourhood dogs with the best steak they would ever eat, and then when they were comfortable with me I had cut off their ears; brought them home; and cured, scudded, de-limed, and tanned them. In the early days it had all been a bit hit and miss, but I was an expert tanner these days and knew exactly how to get the best results. I finally stitched the little pieces of leather together, with a resulting patchwork sofa of varying colours; a veritable kaleidoscope of dog ears. A victory of man over beast.

Did my sofa have fleas? How could that be possible after all the processes involved in producing the leather? I picked up one of the cushions. These were my pride and joy. Every cushion was completely unique, because of course no two animals are the same, and so the mix of ears became my choice, and I opted for chaotic perfection. I stuffed them with the best goose feathers I could find, freshly plucked and sent from Canada. I didn't scrimp on my home comforts.

I plumped the cushion and bent down to return it to its place. As I did so, a low growl emitted from under the sofa. I cocked my head and started to move away, and something abruptly clamped its jaws around my left ankle. I screamed and twisted, but the thing wouldn't let go. I fell backwards, knocking my coffee table and laptop flying. My foot started to disappear under the sofa, something absurdly strong dragging me. I pulled myself backwards on my elbows, the pain in my ankle unbearable as the thing that had me, clenched its grip ever tighter. I couldn't see it, but I could feel the teeth stabbing through my skin and blood oozing around the wound. I lashed out hard with my right leg to try to dislodge it and connected with … nothing.

As suddenly as it had started, the attack was over. I scurried backwards, staring down at my foot. There were no marks. No tearing, no bruising, no blood.

Shivering slightly, I stood up. I pulled the sofa forwards and then tipped it back. Nothing underneath. There were no gaps in the upholstery. Nothing hiding anywhere. I appeared to be completely alone in the apartment.

Perplexed and angry, and in spite of the late hour, I decided to take my anger out to the streets. I donned my long leather jacket and dark jeans and shades and walked with lengthy strides, full of rage. The night people moved instinctively out of my way. I covered my usual route but there were no stray dogs around. I moved farther away from home. Still nothing. I walked for hours until my fury had mellowed into a weary resentment.

Why did the dogs make me do it?

I turned my face to home, my mind full of tired memories of my mother, and all of the foster homes, along with all of the pets in those homes so lavished in love and affection.

As I unlocked my front door, my stomach contracted with a sense of unease. I flashed back to the evening before and frowned. The apartment felt strangely alien. I shook my head, tired. I decided to forgo my shower and simply get some shut eye, but first I headed into the bathroom to wash my face and brush my teeth.

I pushed the door behind me but must have pushed a little harder than I had thought. The door swung out of my grasp and slammed shut, startling me. The bathroom light started to flicker and shimmer. The light dimmed and flashed and then went out altogether. I fumbled around in the dark trying to find the door handle so that I could let myself into the hall and turn the light on there. I couldn't find the handle.

I couldn't find the door.

I located the mirror and then rubbed the wall to the side of it. The door should have been about two steps to the left. I planted my hands on the wall and then recoiled. The walls were warm and soft. What could this be?

Were the walls hairy?

I stood motionless, my eyes wide, trying to pierce the depths of the gloom. A faint glow came from the floor. I looked down at the tiles that fluoresced slightly under my feet. The longer I stared the more I could start to make out the blue strands in the marble. The light from the floor began to grow brighter, throwing the walls into relief. Now I could see that the walls had the same quality and texture of the leathery inside of a dog's ear. Delicate pink tones with strands of hair here and there, the crinkly effect of the cartilage. I could feel warmth emanating from the surfaces.

I stumbled into the middle of the room. The tiles looked like pale skin, a kind of ghastly grey, old parchment. The blue lines looked for all the world like small veins. I watched the veins begin to fill with blood. They grew plump with it, and I could clearly see them pulsing. The floor was lurid now, the veins repulsive, throbbing and swelling, distended and finally with a hiss and a dull popping noise they exploded around me. I screamed in fear and was drenched in warm blood that ran into my eyes and mouth. Heavier clots rained down around me like cannon shot. Terrified, I scooted backwards, slipping and falling to the floor, landing with a soft thud on the slick, unnatural parchment. The room stank, a kind of cloying and meaty stink with a strong metallic undertone. I retched onto the floor, starting to blub as panic took me in its iron grip.

I had to find the door! It had to be here. I had to get out! With difficulty, I pushed myself up and hammered my fists against the spongy and velvety walls. Far too much give. I punched at them and heard a deep, irritated growl. I thumped harder. The growl became louder, more of a snarl. I turned and saw the mirror, hanging surreally on its uncanny background, and snatched it off its hook. I threw it on the floor, but the floor was too soft. I picked it up and smashed it into the bath. I retrieved some of the larger fragments, slicing my fingers as I did so, paying no heed to the pain.

Viciously, I stabbed the fragments into the walls where I knew the door should be. The fragments stuck, and I pulled them out. A scream of rage reverberated around me. The malevolence of the growling and snarling turned my bowels turned to ice. The skin and flesh on my hands were in tatters and gripping the glass was difficult, but again and again I plunged the shards into the wall until with a great bloody belch and a roar, I was expelled from the bathroom into the hallway, landing on my stomach as the door slammed shut behind me.

Shaking uncontrollably, I looked at my hands, fearing the worst.

I was clean. There was no blood.

I stood and reached for the bathroom door handle. There was a low warning growl and silence. I backed away from the door into the living room.

My heart thumped hard in my chest, and I hiccoughed, quietly sobbing but trying to gain control of myself. At a loss, I realised I had no idea what to do or where to turn. I walked through into the kitchen and grabbed a bottle of whisky from the cupboard. I needed to sit and think. The whisky would calm me down. Soothe me.

But as I settled on the sofa, it exploded around me. Feathers from the cushions flew everywhere. The ghosts of the geese they had been plucked from floated through the air like clouds of angel wings. If only that had been the worst of it. What waited for me when the feathers settled originated straight from the depths of hell. Dozens and dozens of dogs had erupted from the sofa like a canine volcano. Big dogs, small dogs, pedigree dogs, mutts and cross breeds, furry, hairy, healthy, starving, old and young; suddenly my room seemed full of living breathing dogs, their eyes shining red with a loathsome and malefic intensity, hackles raised … and all minus their ears. They turned as one towards me, and I watched as their lips curled back over their sharp teeth and they crouched ready to spring. I understood in that moment, just before my mind snapped, that when the dogs had finished with me, it would be my flesh and blood that decorated all that remained of my beloved sofa.

# MAKE DO AND MEND

I peered out from behind the heavy velvet curtains, my face in shadow, my head backlit by the low light burning in the corner of the room behind me. The quiet side street where I lived was in darkness, with the exception of the street lamp at the junction. I watched dry leaves, caught under the halo of light, dance in a sudden breeze, before I satisfied myself that no-one was around, and dropped the curtain back into position.

4.12 am. This night seemed endless. How much longer? I'd had a message to say he would be here after midnight.

I backed up, perched on my worn brocade sofa, my back tall and rigid, then sighed with nerves born of frustration. Slouched. Twiddled with a loose thread on the arm rest. Worried the thread until it came free, and stared down at it in accusatory disappointment. It would never be a part of my sofa again. I couldn't fix it. Couldn't make it right. Could I?

I fiddled. Weaved the thread back into the fraying edge. Pulled it tightly with my fingers, smoothed it down, and then tucked the edges out of sight. With a needle I could camouflage this, no problem.

Make do and mend, my mother used to tell me, much as my grandmother, a teenager during the Second World War, had instructed her. My grandmother, happy and positive, had lived a frugal life. My mother, austere and

51

hard-wired, had been a profligate. I wavered between the two. Bursts of obscene consumerism, intermingled with periods of severe thrift. This had bemused my husband no end.

The doorbell chimed loudly in the darkness, and I bit back a shriek of shock. Heart pounding, intent only on stopping the noise and alerting the neighbours to my devious misdoings, I ran into the dark hall and stopped at the front door. I slid back the deadbolt and turned the key. A man in a filthy waxed jacket stepped inside. He smelt of motorcycle oil and spoilt meat. I gagged and turned away. He closed the door behind himself, hefted his helmet and his rucksack and then twisted towards me. An old, close-knit khaki scarf covered his face, below rheumy eyes.

"Do you have the money?" his muffled voice was low, throaty.

"I do," I stuttered, my own voice sounding unnaturally high-pitched in comparison to his. With my heart in my mouth, we stood and regarded each other.

"Well hand it over, love. I haven't got all night."

I scurried back into the living room. Got on my hands and knees and fished under the sofa. I panicked when I couldn't find the wad of cash. Flailed my arm backwards and forwards, pushing my face close to the dusty smelling upholstery, shoulder jammed against the wood, my rump in the air.

My fingers brushed something. Plastic. Yes. I pushed against the heavy sofa so that it moved backwards, giving me the precious few inches I needed, and scrabbled for the small rectangular package. I drew it towards me, shook the dust away. Practically all of my savings in twenty pound notes were wrapped in a flimsy white pedal bin liner and taped securely.

I backed out and sat on my haunches, blowing my hair back from my face. When I turned, the man was standing in the doorway looking at my backside. The skin around his eyes crinkled. He appeared to be smiling beneath the scarf.

I jumped up and offered him the package. "It's all there. Twenty-eight." I'd paid another two up front. A non-refundable deposit.

He nodded upstairs. "Want to give me a ... tip? You know, for my trouble?" he asked, and I heard the lust, thick in his throat.

I flushed to the roots of my hair and shook my head.

He laughed. It was loud and jolly. I worried again about the neighbours.

I fiddled with my wedding ring, afraid to look at him. His laughter died down.

"Right. So." He sounded cheerful enough. He had his money. My money. I guess he had earned it. He opened his rucksack and pulled out a brown paper package tied with string, the old fashioned way, which he placed on the floor. It was larger than I'd expected, well over a foot in length and five inches across. It was well wrapped. He stuffed his money inside the vacuum he had created in his bag, then picked the parcel up and handed it to me. "We're done then."

I nodded, my throat dry. He let himself out of the front door. I stuffed the parcel under one arm, surprised by its heaviness, and carefully bolted the door after him. Alone again. Relief.

I stood for some time in the gloomy hall. The only light came from the muted lamp in the living room. I waited for the energy in the house to settle. It was unnerving for another person—and a man at that—to occupy this space, usually solely mine. It had been a while since I had entertained visitors.

My heart was still pounding. I looked at the door. Listened for the sound of a motorcycle roaring away into the distance, but heard nothing. I thought of the man's crinkled eyes. Remembered how he had been looking at me. I wondered what his face had looked like underneath the scarf. Had he really wanted to…?

Absurd. But the thought of a man desiring me again. It felt good.

Should I have? I ran the film in my head. Pictured him shedding his clothes in the hall. Following me upstairs, tearing at my clothes. Imagined a frantic, hard coupling. My legs wrapped around him, his big, filthy hands under my rump, pulling me to him, my breasts squashed against his chest, my teeth nipping at his shoulder. Him grunting, me gasping.

I shook my head clear. Breathed deeply. Too late now. He had gone. I didn't want to see him again. And in any case, I had to consider my husband.

I took the parcel through to the kitchen, down a few steps at the back of the house. I needed to be careful in here. The kitchen was overlooked by the neighbours' kitchen to my right. I moved easily in the dark and located the cords to pull the blinds closed. I had years of familiarity with the layout of the house and everything within it. When I felt certain I couldn't be observed by any outsiders, I flicked the main kitchen lights on and blinked in the sudden aggressive brightness. My eyes were far from ready for daylight, and I felt momentarily displaced, as though I had been travelling long haul.

I picked out a sharp knife from the draining board and sliced through the string that bound the parcel together, then carefully peeled back the brown paper from its contents. A heavy-duty black plastic bag formed the next layer. I unrolled the bag. *Boyles Butchers: Compleat Meat* read the legend. Had Boyles Butchers been the company who had fulfilled this order for me, I wondered? No way of knowing of course. It had all been anonymous. Over the internet. Friend of a friend, kind of thing.

I reached into the bag and pulled the object out. Now I had a layer of bubble wrap to contend with. I picked the knife up again. Sliced the tape. Unrolled the object from the wrap, until at last one final layer remained. Tissue paper. Neatly folded. White. Unblemished. Pristine.

How could that be? Given what had to be done to the object?

I hadn't expected such a professional finish. This … gift wrapping.

But it was a gift. It was special. To me.

I stared down at the discards on the table, trying not to focus on the shape of the object itself. My eyes were stinging and my limbs were heavy. I felt slightly nauseous. No sleep and too much caffeine. It was well after five in the morning. The soft light of dawn wouldn't be far away. The snowy tissue paper reminded me that this was a moment to be cherished. I shouldn't proceed until I warranted this gift, until I was worthy of the moment.

I cleared the rubbish away, picked up my expensive prize, and carried it carefully upstairs. First I would sleep, and then, suitably refreshed, I would open my parcel.

\*\*\*

I awoke at around three in the afternoon. I liked to sleep with the window open, and in the distance I could hear traffic and a few birds twittering in the tree across the road. Light filtered through my curtains. I was disoriented for a moment. Asleep in the daytime? Then I remembered why and shivered.

I rolled onto my side and stared at the void that my husband Matthew had once occupied. Ten months since his accident. He had been knocked over on a crossing when he nipped out to buy a loaf of bread. He'd been brain dead the moment his head had smashed the windscreen of the car.

After twenty years of his constant companionship, I found it tough to be alone. I had given permission for the hospital to use whatever organs of his body were deemed useful before we switched off his life support. The relatives had been profoundly grateful, I'd had letters thanking me, telling me what a difference he had made to their lives. That had been some consolation, but not much.

What about me? What about everything I had lost? Everything he had been to me? Friend, confidant, partner in crime, chief cook, bottle washer. Lover.

Raw grief had slowly given way to an unbearable loneliness. And at forty-three, I considered myself far from being 'over the hill'. Bold friends gently suggested me I might meet somebody new, but somebody new wasn't him, was it? I missed him, missed every part of him, especially his touch. He had fulfilled me with just a gentle stroke, his hand on my skin. It had been nothing and yet it had been everything.

I sat up and swung myself out of bed with a renewed sense of purpose. Time to get busy. The object, still wrapped in its cotton fresh tissue paper was lying innocuously on my dressing table. I ran my fingers lightly across it.

Soon.

***

A flurry of activity.

I stripped my bed and remade it with fresh linen. I ran a duster over the surfaces, tidied clothes away, bundled used underwear into the clothes basket. I took the bedside rug downstairs and shook it heartily out of the back door, returned to plump pillows, vacuum and spray a gloriously expensive bergamot room fragrance into the air.

Satisfied that the room was clean and welcoming, I considered myself. When had I last eaten? I didn't feel particularly hungry, but it seemed like a good idea. I poked around, unenthusiastically, in the kitchen cupboards before settling on a tin of soup. If nothing else this would line my stomach and prevent any grumbles later.

I washed the pots and checked the doors and windows were all locked and bolted. I unplugged the house phone. I didn't need to worry about my mobile, I never bothered charging it anymore. There was no-one I wanted to hear from.

It was time to tidy myself up. It had been a long while since I had bothered with anything more than a perfunctory shower and hair wash. Tonight would be different however. Tonight, finally, I wanted to shine. I wanted to look and smell and feel the way that Matthew would expect.

I started with my feet, trimmed my toenails, and exfoliated my heels. Then worked on my fingernails. They were short and functional. I tidied them up, my nail file rasping busily back and forth while I hummed to myself. Better.

Defuzzing was surprisingly fun. It had been so long; I hadn't realised the extent to which I had let myself go. My legs and underarms were quickly seen to, but I took a small pair of scissors to my pubic hair before setting to with a razor. I didn't like a complete absence of hair down there, and I wasn't agile or creative enough to trim a landing strip, but I did like short and tidy. Matthew had appreciated this too. He had run his hands up and down my body, nuzzled me with his warm face, basked in my soft smoothness in comparison to his muscular coarseness.

I remained in the shower for an age. Washing my hair in apple scented shampoo, rinsing and then conditioning with a matching product. I massaged my scalp, enjoying the sensation of the small spiky hairs at the roots under my fingertips. I soaped myself all over with expensive bubbles and rubbed an exfoliating mitt across my skin, sloughing off the dead skin and rinsing it down the drain, wishing I could do that with my memories. Once finished, I was hot and pink. I perched on the edge of the bath to cool down, wrapped in a big towel, and carefully combed my hair through, before drying it with my curling tongs and styling myself pretty.

Back in my bedroom, I reverently lifted the package from the dressing table and placed it on the centre of my bed. I felt excited now as I moved around, naked, making last minute preparations. I lit a scented candle and positioned it on my bedside table. I rubbed body lotion into my skin, careful to make sure I kneaded it into every nook and cranny, every curve, every hollow, softening skin which had become pale and dry without anyone to appreciate it over the past long months alone.

I applied a little mascara. Only twenty-four hours ago my eyes had been swollen and dull, now they were wide open and sparkling. I added a little coloured lip gloss and pinched my cheeks to make them flush a little more.

I stood and looked at myself in the mirror, saw myself as a goddess, paying homage to the man she loved.

One final touch. Anointment. In the bottom of my bedside cabinet I kept a small bottle of oil that worked beautifully as a lube. I sat back on the bed, poured some onto my fingers and opened my legs. I rubbed the oil into the folds of my vagina. My lips were already swelling with anticipation. I felt an instant tingle of arousal as my fingers slipped and slid gently around. I'd forgotten what the sensation. I lingered there, gently circling my clitoris. So good.

I rubbed the remaining oil into my breasts. I'd lost some weight, but my breasts were still full, if not as firm as they had once been. I rolled my nipples between finger and thumb, the oil lending a lovely silkiness to the action. My nipples sprung to life, proud to the touch. I moaned softly, desire washing through me.

Shaking with anticipation, I reached across to the package, my fingers leaving oily fingerprints on the virgin tissue paper as I finally ripped the parcel open.

It had been so long. Too long. I hadn't wanted to touch myself. It felt disloyal to Matthew somehow to engage in any sort of sexual activity without him. And so I had moved heaven and earth to bring Matthew back to me. I had met someone online who could farm body parts from the cadavers of those whose bodies had been donated to science, as Matthew had. £10,000 had brought me a body part easily enough. The extra £20,000 had been spent on mummification to my exact and specific requirements.

Hidden in the tissue paper was Matthew's right arm, cut off below the elbow. Some faceless orderly or medical student had cut Matthew's arm free from the rest of him and delivered it to the next anonymous person in the chain, maybe Mr Boyle the 'compleat meat' butcher. A modern pair of Burke and Hare's. The flesh was dark now, a rich mahogany, thanks to the process it had been put through by my unnamed contact on the internet. The arm was solid, but with a little give. A kind of leather dildo perhaps. I'd asked particularly to have the middle finger set slightly out of line with the others and the little finger—surplus to my requirements—removed altogether. The thumb curved down and round slightly. It looked perfect in theory. I had known it would be. It was time to put it into practice.

I lay back on the bed, parted my legs once more. Clasping Matthew's arm above the wrist, I gently stroked myself with his middle finger. It felt good. I moved the hand down. His finger slipped inside me, as easily as it ever had, the stiff fingers on either side stroked my labia, his thumb caressed my pubis. It was familiar. Home.

Closing my eyes, Matthew joined me once more. I could feel his weight next to me when he shifted to kneeling. He always liked to watch me as my excitement grew. If I opened my eyes, his cock would be swaying slightly, just out of the grasp of my greedy mouth. I parted my lips, felt the warmth of him so close, flicked my tongue out to catch him. Deeper his finger explored inside me, my clitoris warm and swollen under his palm, my juices slick. His hand moved up and down, his middle finger in and out of me, rubbing, tormenting me. I ground myself against his hand. He pushed back. I cried out in ecstasy.

How I had missed his touch.

# MANAGING MURDER

The day after I lost my house, I sat on a single bed with a thin mattress in a cheap and musty hotel room, twisting my wedding ring around and around my finger, my veins burning as though flowing with corrosive acid. Anger and hatred bubbled inside me like the fetid contents of an evil cauldron. The walls were thin so I remained mute, but mentally I howled like a banshee, long and loud and out of control, primeval in my distress.

My doctor had given me pills to offset some of the extreme anxiety, but they didn't work instantly. I had to wait for them to kick in and for all this inner turbulence to subside before I could feel relatively in control.

But I doubted I would ever feel sane again.

Four months ago I had been called to my manager's office, and I turned up, shining and smiling, hopeful of promotion. I considered Ryan Eads not a friend exactly, but an ally in a difficult world of greed, corruption, and backstabbing. When his job had been at risk, I pulled out all the stops to ensure his application for his own post was backed up by intelligent documentation and well thought-out strategy. His submission was innovative, creative, passionate, and direct, and in large part, that was thanks to me. They had given him a hard time at the interview of course; his superiors probably wanted someone new, but there could be no denying how good an internal candidate he actually was. He also had hard-hitting external contacts worth good money to the company. They offered him his job.

But when my turn came to interview for my post, I wasn't offered my job.

My application was good of course, but my interview was shaky, and I had been singled out as a 'difficult member of staff' even before I walked into the interview room. My cards were marked. Sitting opposite Ryan, listening to his feedback, my mouth dropped open.

What he said made absolutely no sense.

But he was talking to me.

And in English.

"Rude," he said. "Abrasive. Intellectually intimidating."

Okay, I was not given to suffering fools gladly, and the organisation was full of them. I was impatient, no doubt about that. I had a tendency to tell people if I found them wanting in some way. Well, sometimes they needed to be told.

"Come on," I said to him, "I'm good at what I do. I bring out the best in people." But he only shook his head.

He was questioning my ability to get on with people, but actually it seemed what he wanted was someone who kowtowed to the regime the institution was developing. I frowned, my eyes pricked with tears. I had known this man for four years, but now anger and fear were bubbling up inside me and he felt like a stranger. We had worked together closely and in that time, I'd brought together disparate groups of employees to work for the greater good of the organisation and the results always reflected well on him. I understood these people, our colleagues, recognised their challenges and what they were trying to achieve. I took time to get to know them, built bridges that reached them. They respected me because I was honest with them. How could he suggest I didn't get on with them?

"No, you're hard to work with," he continued. "Your colleagues don't like you."

My stomach dropped into my shoes.

"They don't like me?" The very idea of this tapped into something buried deep within me. I wanted to be liked. *What's wrong with me?* "Nobody has ever said anything or intimated," I petered out, full of doubt. Colleagues smiled with me, laughed with me, chatted. *Are they being false? Am I deluded? Am I incapable of reading social situations correctly?*

He merely shrugged. I wondered if he knew how hurtful this conversation was to me.

He went on, but I couldn't digest what he was saying. I think he cast doubt on my ability to do key parts of my job. I alternated between fury and shame as I listened to him. He made no mention of the effort and the energy I had put in to my job. He failed to note the creativity, the innovation, the enterprising ideas, the ways and means by which I had pulled our department together. I had ensured that what *we* did was a success. His one-sided diatribe against me should have seemed laughable, but I was completely bewildered. Worst of all, I started to distrust myself.

He finished by noting that the company would now have to advertise externally, and I would be required to slip backward into a lesser role. They would find something for me to do. My mind began to turn inwards. I looked down the long black corridor to my soul. It was a bleak journey.

"I can't do that!" I blurted in panic. "I can't watch someone else do a job which I already do so well. You know they'll do it worse than me. And I won't do the job for them if they can't do it! Not if they get paid better money for it than me in my 'lesser role'."

"You could take redundancy," he said calmly. Dispassionately.

My stomach knotted. My betrayal was complete. He recognised no value in me. He wanted to release my salary to pay for the new external post. He didn't want to keep me. My emotions felt like a dried out rubber band, stretched too far and about to snap. I had to get out, get away from him, get away from the colleagues that I had liked and trusted, some that I had considered friends. Just get away.

That night I felt my failure acutely. I sobbed into my pillow. I wished for death. Felt the shame that would reflect on my husband, on my family. I felt worthless. The night was long and black, and with every in-breath my soul grew darker and my thoughts more muddled.

\*\*\*

I never returned to work. Financial worries placed pressures on my relationship with my husband. Without my salary, we could not afford the mortgage and defaulted. We had to sell the house in a rush, and we lost money on it. My husband couldn't cope with my anxiety and depression and sought solace elsewhere. In the end, we called it quits. He moved on. I moved into a cheap and miserable hotel and spent hours sitting on the bed feeling miserable, replaying that final conversation with Ryan over and over and over again in my head, weeping and desperate for respite.

Feeling pain. Feeling bitterness. Feeling hatred. Feeling lonely.

Lonely apart from the voices, that is. My inner voices were busy swirling in and out of my consciousness. The final conversation with Ryan looped in my mind and the voices kept it company. One small voice, a kind voice, tried to keep me calm and rational, but it was drowned out in a swell of anger and loathing, voices hurt by Ryan's savage betrayal, by colleagues ripe with indifference.

*It isn't fair, it isn't fair, it isn't fair.* That voice beat like a drum in my temples.

'So what if it isn't fair?" I answered. "It's life. I can't do anything about it!"

*You can do something about it!* The voice whispered. *Take control back! Teach him a lesson. Teach everyone a lesson.*

"I can't! What can I do? I'm nothing now. I'm a failure."

*Be proactive. Look for new work?* The placatory voice; rational, calm.

"Who has he spoken to? Who has he told this stuff to? My reputation is ruined."

*Teach him a lesson.*
*Do something. Anything.*
*Teach him a lesson.*
*You're a failure.*
*Teach him a lesson!*
*At least try.*

Teach him a lesson? What did the voices know? But it was food for thought and gradually they began to win me around. I listened to them. Well they were right. I couldn't just do nothing. I had always been a dynamic go-getting individual. It was what made me a success at my job in the first place.

The voices just kept on and on at me. Every moment, waking or unconscious. After one particularly troubled night, I awoke with a start, the word *Kill!* ringing in my ears. For a moment I thought I had company, someone bending over and talking low in my ear, but as I cast around the room I could neither see nor hear anyone.

My heart beat hard in my chest. Damn Ryan.

*Why should he be out enjoying life, talking crap with everyone he comes across and smiling smugly at his wife in restaurants, when you now have so little?*

But, to kill, I'd never get away with that.

*You don't know until you try.*

That's crazy.

*Think about it.*

No!

\*\*\*

But of course I did think about it. I dreamt up dramatic endings for Ryan. It was so much more satisfying than contemplating ending my own life.

And so, finally, I had an interest in something. I visited the library for inspiration drawn from books about murder, both solved and unsolved. I watched endless re-runs of *CSI* and *Law and Order*. I quickly realised that the drawback with only killing one person and planning a murder in advance, was that this made it much more likely that I would be caught very quickly. I could imagine the scenario. Detectives interviewing Ryan's wife: "Mrs Eads, did anyone have a grudge against your husband? Any disgruntled ex-employees for example?"

"Why now that you come to mention it detective, there was that awful Laurel Williams. No-one liked her."

And clunk! They would have me locked up faster than Usain Bolt off the starting blocks.

I turned my attention to the serial killer section of the bookshelf. To kill more than one person while secretly actually targeting just one, well it's not an entirely new concept is it? But motiveless murder has the advantage that it makes things more difficult for the police.

As long as you're not seen and don't leave too many clues behind, I suppose. That's the tough bit.

*You can do this.*

I guess maybe it's feasible.

*You need to be clever about it.*

I am clever.

*Who's first then?*

\*\*\*

She was the duty manager in a fast food burger restaurant. After I had spent fifteen minutes queuing up for a burger, I had a pretty good idea that if I had to work for her I would want to kill her. Fast food? Was she kidding? She had six kids managing the tills, with three 'runners' (and I use this term sarcastically) collecting together the components of people's meals. There were maybe another three members of staff flipping burgers and shaking fries behind her, and she still couldn't serve the eight people in front of me and give me the correct burger in less than a quarter of an hour.

She never smiled at a customer or colleague once the whole time I stood there. There was no direction for those serving and only an occasional shouted order at the workers in the kitchen. When I pointed out the mistake in my burger, she looked at me blankly and fetched another one without uttering a single nicety or apology. Instead she spouted the words that she had been instructed to repeat like the dullest automaton: "Enjoy your meal. Who's next please?"

The restaurant closed at ten that evening. I waited outside wearing my nondescript black wool coat with the hood up, my hands deep in my pockets. Her colleagues left one by one, and she stayed on alone, cashing up and doing whatever restaurant managers do at the end of their shifts.

She exited through the back door at around 10:45 pm, setting the alarm and turning off the lights as she went. I had figured that employees parked their cars around the back, and I was right. There was little light in the car park. The gloom was perfect for me. I was ready. I took my right hand out of my pocket and stabbed her twice with the large kitchen knife I had secreted there by slitting the bottom of my pocket.

I think I stabbed her once in the stomach and once in the chest. There was more resistance with the chest. She cried out and fell onto her knees immediately, one hand clutching her breast. I considered stabbing her again, but then she fell face down, one hand outstretched towards me. It opened and closed for a while, scrabbled at the dirt, and was still.

I bent down and looked at her. Studied the one dark eye I could see. Was there anything going on in her mind? I couldn't tell. I don't know how long I was there. Long enough for the blood spreading out from her to become a large, dark puddle. I inhaled her scent, stale perfume and chip fat, then dabbled my finger in the blood.

I reached into my other pocket and pulled out the cold and greasy box of fries I had bought from her restaurant earlier. Sprinkling them over her, I stuffed the packet back into my pocket. I was too clever to leave fingerprints of course.

I walked away, quickly but not at running pace. I didn't want to draw attention to myself. Once beyond the confines of the restaurant and car park, I melted down a side road and found my car. I drove back to my hotel room. I didn't even break into a sweat.

Later I sat on my bed, mulling it over. Marvelling. The voices in my head were largely ecstatic and congratulatory. Group hugs all round.

*It was easy.*

*Very easy.*

The police could still come knocking.

*No, we're home free.*

*We did it! She was a good choice. Managers need to learn they can't treat their employees so poorly.*

*We showed her.*

*We taught her a lesson.*

*You need to stop. This isn't right.*

*They're not going to look for us. An ordinary woman with no ties to the restaurant manager.*

I was hyper. Couldn't sleep. Didn't even try. I perched on my bed, listening to the voices in my head. The placatory, rational voice seemed to be growing fainter. Maybe the others were eating her. Maybe she was convinced they were right.

My next concern was about how we were going to move from the restaurant manager to Ryan, our ultimate goal. It was some bizarre version of five degrees of separation.

*They have to be linked in some way.*

*But not in a way that comes back to us.*

*They can't be five people whom we know.*

*Oh it's going to be five people is it?*

*How many murders do you have to do to be a serial killer?*

*We didn't know her anyway.*

*So how do we link her to the next one?*

*And where do we find the next one?*

*And when?*

*Don't worry. They'll find us. The ones who need our assistance. We can make them better people. Nicer people.*

*Or at least we can stop them from hurting others.*
*Other employees who work so hard.*
*Yes.*
Yes. That's all I wanted.

***

Several days later I was back in the library studying some more books and techniques. According to the internet, three or more murders, or sometimes just two or more, made you a serial killer. The rule was they had to be over a period of time and have breaks in between. I was sure I could manage that. I needed to consider my options and that would take time.

Thinking time.

Most serial killers had a modus operandi, an MO, apparently. I'd heard that phrase bandied around on crime dramas too. I certainly didn't want to get involved in anything sexual. Ick. I wanted nice, clean murders. The killings had to be linked in some way without directly pointing at me. As long as most of them were motiveless, just people I took a dislike to, that would help, right? But I had to have a signature of some kind.

I pondered that one carefully.

In the meantime, I had to find myself somewhere new to live. The hotel, as grim as it was, was a complete drain on my finances. I started looking around for a small studio and that was when I found victim number two.

***

Jane Winters was the office manager at a property rental agency. She was everything I hated in a female manager. Blonde, young, and slim. She packed her curves into tight pencil skirts, tucking her tailored, expensive, and slightly see-through blouse into them. She wore five inch heels and clip-clopped around the office like a pony, her hair swinging in an affected way as she moved. She hadn't made it to her lofty position in the company through her welcoming and sunny personality that was for sure. Her smile never made it to her eyes. She gave nothing of herself away, spread no cheer, cracked no jokes. She was efficient but as cold as a polar bear's testicles.

I only went into the office once, just to register my interest in a property. After that I simply phoned up. If she answered the phone, she would inform me that there was nothing suitable for me, and I would be dismissed within thirty seconds. I felt my sense of injustice mounting every time I spoke to her. She was working. I wasn't. She was genuinely horrible to people. I wasn't.

She needed to be taught a lesson.

In accordance with my desire to be anonymous, I realised I didn't want to be a regular at the agency, so I stopped contacting them. I found a studio apartment via another agency, but I kept in touch with Ms Winters by following her around.

*Stalking her.*

She worked 9 to 5:30 at the office most days and rarely stayed late. Then she would go home to a lavish house on the outskirts of town with a large garden maintained by an external company. She lived with a well-to-do, good-looking man.

*Nice suits!*

*Nice Lotus!*

*Nice security cameras. Let's not get too close.*

*Worth a small fortune.*

*It's so unfair that they have all this!*

*Do something about them and their smug arrogance!*

Occasionally, back at work, she needed to show someone around a house or apartment, I guess if members of her team were sick or on holiday. It was this that provided me with my best chance. Observing closely, I noticed that the pattern of a house visit was always the same. She would arrive first and enter the property. Shew would then greet the visitor when they arrived. When the visitor left, she would disappear back into the property, probably to lock it all up, and then return to her car. I would need to take my opportunity as it presented itself.

It presented itself perfectly. One sunny afternoon she made her way to a small house close to a busy road. I drove past and parked some distance away. My heart thumping in anticipation, I twisted my rear view mirror to watch. I waited for the viewer to turn up. They were late. Eventually a young couple did show, they knocked and entered the property. I flipped the hood of my coat up and walked nonchalantly back to the house. As luck would have it there was a little alley on the side. I hid behind a dustbin.

After twenty minutes, the couple left the property. I could hear Jane Winters asking them to call her as soon as they made up their minds, and saying how lovely it was to have met them.

*Blah blah blah.*

*She doesn't mean any of it.*

*Sentimental nonsense.*

As soon as the couple walked away, I headed out of the alley and tapped on the front door. I wanted to smile I was so happy.

I heard Jane's feet clip-clopping on the wooden floorboards beyond the door. "Did you forget something?" she asked and swung the door open.

I was ready. I pushed through and at her. My momentum, her surprise, and I guess her ridiculous shoes, made her unsteady. She cried out in alarm as she fell backwards. In one movement I was able to push the front door closed behind me and use it as a springboard to leap forward onto her. I fished my knife out of my pocket. It snarled in the lining, giving Jane a chance to attempt an escape. She didn't do that. Instead she opened her mouth to scream. I slapped her with as much force as I could muster, and her head rocked sideways. She started to blub. The knife finally came free, and I stabbed at her chest. Jane tried to scrabble backwards, and I struck her hip. Neither of those wounds were going to kill her.

She breathed in so that she could try to scream again.

The adrenaline flowed through me. I couldn't let her make a noise. I stabbed at her wildly, aiming for her mouth. Anything to shut her up. Again and again. She fought back. I stabbed at her fingers, her hands, her arms, her shoulders. The knife went into her and out, over and over. Sometimes it met resistance, sometimes it slid in easily. The hall was red. All I could see was red.

The world stilled. My breathing slowed down. I sat back on my haunches and stared at what I had done. The walls were dotted with spots of blood that had flown everywhere in the frenzy. Blood was pooling on the floor around her body and was smeared all over the floorboards where we had struggled. Jane's white blouse was now a red shredded rag. Her blonde hair was slick with blood and flesh. Her face was unrecognisable. Her teeth grinned at me through a lipless mouth.

I was covered in her blood too. There had been no avoiding it. This was a messy scene. She had fought hard. My footprints and handprints were everywhere. I couldn't leave this amount of evidence behind me.

I stood, feeling like an old woman. My shoulders, arms, thighs, and hands were aching from restraining the mad woman on the floor in front of me. I avoided her sightless gaze. Stepped over her. Walked through to the back of the house.

The house was being let semi-furnished so there were some items around. In the kitchen I found a bucket. I let myself out into the yard and found a hard brush used on patios. There was no soap or detergent anywhere, but I did find toilet bleach in the utility space. I ran the water in the kitchen and flung it and the bleach about the hall. I scrubbed at the floor and the walls until everything turned pink and my hand and footprints couldn't be seen

For my final act, I sprinkled Jane's body with a large portion of cold, greasy fries that I had brought along especially for the occasion. My brand new MO.

Genius.

I stayed in the house, sitting quietly in the kitchen, until darkness fell, and then I slipped out the back, down the alley and returned to my car. Once back at my studio I stripped off, placed all of my clothes in a bin liner and scrubbed myself clean in the shower. I then popped out again and disposed of my clothes in a dumpster downtown before buying a pizza and eating the whole thing while sitting on my bed.

But something bothered me.

*We have a thing against women?*

*No. Sheesh! Women rock!*

*It looks like we hate them!*

*We need to target a man.*

*That Winters bitch was hard work!*

*So how do we know we can take on a man?*

Winters had been a small, slim woman, but I was going to feel the strain in my shoulders, and my hands particularly, for a few days. Ryan was a man in his early fifties who worked out. *How was I going to subdue him so that I could set about doing what I wanted to do?*

I gave it some thought.

*** 

Several weeks later I was wandering around Bigelow's hypermarket when I happened upon my next victim. He was probably a nice guy, but he was a manager, and he was far too young. He was making managerial decisions, ordering employees about who probably had more years' experience than he'd had Christmas dinners. And he still had pimples.

He annoyed me on sight.

For the next few weeks I hung around watching the employees' entrance at Bigelow's. This was a greater challenge than the burger restaurant because there were more employees coming and going, and more security. I found out which was the kid's car however, a modest three-year-old Ford, nothing flashy, and was pleased by his tendency to park at the rear of the employees' car park near some scrubland with large thorny bushes.

I equipped myself with a new, thick, black coat and hood and made the necessary adjustments to the right hand pocket so that I could get my knife, freshly sharpened, in and out without it snagging on anything. I lined the left-hand pocket with plastic so that I could keep the fries in there without them staining the outside of the coat with grease, or making it smell. I'd bought new boots; cheap, Chinese manufactured, on sale everywhere and two sizes too big. I tied my hair back and hid it under a black net. I had my new weapon. I was ready.

Every night as soon as it was dark, I made my way on foot to the scrubland at the back of Bigelow's and hid among the thorny bushes. I waited for the kid to come out. I had to abandon what I was doing for a few nights in a row, twice when he gave a colleague a ride home and once when the moon was so bright that I couldn't hide effectively.

*He's a nice guy.*

*Generous.*

*We can't worry about that.*

At last, the conditions were right.

He was alone and walked towards his car. When he was close enough, I called out to him.

"Sir? Oh sir? Could you help me please?"

He turned. Cocked his head. Looked towards where I was hiding in the bushes.

"Sir? Could you help? I'm hurt bad."

At that he came towards me.

"Ma'am? Where are you? Shall I call the police?"

"Could you help me first?" Ah the duplicitous joy of being a damsel in distress.

"I'm coming. Where—"

I swung a black bag containing a standard house brick at his head. It connected with a dull crump; the sound of an egg having its top caved in. The kid fell like a stone. Maybe he was dead then. I don't know. I wasn't about to give him mouth to mouth. I dragged him by the arms, pulled him back under cover of the bushes. I took my knife and stabbed him hard, approximately where I considered his heart to be. Blood bubbled out of his chest but there wasn't much of it.

I was pleased.

I sprinkled my fries over him, collected my belongings and slipped away under cover of the night.

*Dead?*
*Dead.*
*That was easy!*
*Pleasing.*
*Little mess.*
*No fuss.*
*No repercussions.*
*No one knocking at the door.*
*Another manager bites the dust.*

The media were all over the killings now, particularly of Ms Winters as that had been hideous, even I agreed with that, but let's face it, the world was better off without her. As I had wished, the murders were being connected, and the media had labelled them 'The Fries Murders'.

*How very imaginative.*
*No matter.*
*A means to an end.*

\*\*\*

I wanted to check just once more that my brick weapon was sound, so next I chose a bank manager, slightly paunchy and in his forties, smart suits, smart car, smart house. I decided to stalk him at his house this time because his workplace was far too exposed. As luck would have it, he had a long driveway with a great deal of shrubbery and trees in the front so that the house could not be seen from the road. He lived alone.

*Divorced maybe.*
*Lonely.*
*Oh how our heart breaks for him.*
*Not.*

I didn't even bother with subterfuge. I just waited for

him to pull up. He stepped out of his car to see what a woman wanted from him at that time of the evening, and I hit him with the bag containing my brick.

He fell to his knees, and I kicked him over, flat on the ground, with my too-large Chinese boots. I hit him once more with the bag, and the strap broke, but he lay still. I stabbed him through the heart and in the stomach. I watched the blood gurgle out and pool around him. I bent over his head, watched his eyes, waited for the light to dim or go out or something, but they kind of just stayed the same. His eyes were grey. The pupils were large. He looked like a fish. I shuddered.

*We hate fish.*

When I was sure he was dead, I threw my fries on him, pocketed the carton and made my way home.

My heart was light. The time had come. I had laid the basis of 'The Fries Murders' and could now turn my attention to getting the revenge I so badly desired. I put my feelers out among old contacts in a general gossipy kind of way. I needed to know what Ryan Eads was going to be up to over the next few weeks and months.

It was difficult. He attended a large number of business meetings all over the place, sometimes taking the train, sometimes driving, sometimes flying. The fact that he stayed in hotels was a problem; I had an aversion to their security measures.

The general vicinity where the office was based was also a no go. I was too well known and would be recognised instantly. I did a little surveillance but was wary of being spotted. Then, as luck would have it, I had a lucky break.

Ryan, always serious about exercise, changed from using his regular inner-city gym to a leisure centre on the outskirts of town. It was a new and exclusive development, sprawling across part of the old green belt, with an impressive array of playing fields and outside courts. Subscription cost a fortune but he probably had access to it courtesy of the company. It had plenty of parking, dotted around the numerous outbuildings that housed squash courts, indoor tennis courts and even dance studios. It was a huge, sparkly, health nut's paradise and Ryan was drawn to it like a fly to a corpse.

Three nights a week I followed him to this Complex of Eternal Youth. The time he arrived varied depending on how long his day had been and where he had travelled to and from. On occasional evenings he would meet a friend and play squash, but mostly he liked to cycle in the velodrome. I hid in the shadows and watched him patiently.

*Stay prepared.*

*Be ready.*

*The time will come.*

*Soon.*

And it did. One evening he arrived in the middle of a torrential downpour. He raced into the main reception area and spoke to a woman on reception. A little later he exited from the main changing area in his squash clothes, carrying a racquet and an umbrella.

Wearing my customary dark clothes and too big boots, I followed Ryan to the squash courts, hugging the dark shadows that swallowed the areas outside the ring of sodium lighting. My breathing was low and even, my footsteps quiet and confident. Ryan went in, I hung back, but through the glass I could see him playing against himself. He worked up a sweat, dashing around the court, hitting the little ball harder and harder, maybe getting the anguish of the day out of his system.

*We can help him with that.*

After thirty minutes or so I saw him mopping himself with his towel. His hair was plastered against his forehead, his face pink, his eyes shining. He looped the towel over his shoulders, picked up his umbrella and racquet and turned towards the exit.

The complex was much quieter this evening with only the indoor courts attracting those hardy enough to come out on such a dreary night. There were very few people around. I moved right away from the squash court, back into the shadows among the trees and shrubs of the exquisitely maintained complex parkland. Ryan came trotting out, down the path towards me. I stepped towards him.

"Ryan," I called. "Ryan."

He stopped in his tracks. Looked my way. "Hello?"

"Ryan? Could you help me please?"

He took a step towards me, squinting through the bright light shining in his eyes, beyond into the darkness where I stood.

"Who is it?"

"It's me! I need your help. Please?"

He walked towards me; his head moving in silhouette like a puzzled dog. I backed away from him right into the darkness behind me. He stumbled on the wet ground. "Hurry!" I called, and he moved a little faster.

I was ready. I swung my bag and hit him square on the side of the head. His glasses flew off and away from us. He didn't fall but bent over clutching his left temple. Blood was seeping between his fingers. He started to straighten up so I swung again. This time his hand was in the way and the crunching noise and terrible yell of anguish suggested I had broken a finger or two. Memories of Jane Winters came flooding back to me. I had to shut Ryan up quickly. Hopefully the rain was drowning out the noise he was making. Using all my strength, I swung the bag with the brick once more and caught Ryan on the rear of the skull. He went down.

Gleefully I watched him. His eyes were trying to focus on me, but he was struggling to stay conscious.

*Stay with us for a little longer Ryan.*

*We enjoy your company.*

*We're friendly.*

*A proper people's person.*

I dragged him to the very edge of the pool of light so that he could see me and so that I could delight in his expression.

"Laurel," he murmured. "Is it you?"

"Hello Ryan," I said brightly. "How are you doing?"

"Why?" he asked.

"Why?" I repeated, and my blood bubbled, acidic black tar in my veins and stomach, bile rising in my mouth. I looked into his eyes and knew all he was seeing was my hatred.

*Take his eyes!*

*The eyes judged us to suit himself!*

*Take his tongue!*

*For the lies he told about us!*

*The lies he told himself to justify not keeping you on the team!*

*Kill him!*

I couldn't kill him with any objectivity. I wasn't cold, dispassionate, or uncaring. I was hot and emotional, full of loathing. And I wanted him dead.

I stabbed him in the stomach, the blade punching through his stomach easily, and he grunted like an animal. The blood flew back up at my face as I wrenched out the knife. The wound instantly bubbled and bled. He moved his hands instinctively to protect himself. I stabbed him in the chest, and he moaned. His head lifted off the grass and I relished the plea I could see in his eyes.

I smiled at him then stabbed his chest again. The knife stuck, and I yanked it, hard. His head fell back, his throat exposed. His mouth worked silently, his eyes blinking in the light as the rain fell around us. I knelt near him. The wet grass, or maybe it was blood, soaked into my black trousers. I watched his eyes. Leaned right into him to breathe against his cheek.

"I was always there for you," I said. "Always loyal. And I'm here for you now." His mouth stopped moving. He shuddered once. His eyes stared blankly at the black sky and rain began to pool there, like tears. He was dead.

*You were never grateful.*
*You should have been grateful.*
*You should have rewarded us*
*Not subjected us to a witch hunt.*
*Not cast us out into the unknown.*

I dragged him back into the darkness and wiped my knife on the grass to clean it. I toyed with the idea of cutting his eyes and tongue out, but to be honest I didn't want to get that intimate. I stood above him, reaching into my pocket for the carton of fries, meaningless except for their link to the first murder.

And then he moved.

I stared down at him, shocked. *He was still alive? How could that be so?*

I scuttled back into the bushes looking for my bag. For long moments I couldn't see it. There it was. Yes. The strap was broken. I hoisted the brick out and moved quickly back to the body. There was movement. Not much, he wasn't going anywhere fast, but I couldn't run the risk of him being found, taken to hospital and then living to tell people that I had hurt him.

I smashed his face with the brick. His nose broke, and

his lips split. With the second blow, I dislodged several teeth. The third one cracked his left eye socket. After that I just kept going. Hollow cracking noises turned to slick, wet, sticky sounds. The brick fell to pieces in my hand. Blood and flesh spattered around me and ran down my face. It ran in my mouth; I was tasting his blood. I threw my head back and let the rain do its best to wash it away. I roared triumphantly at the sky. Over! It was over.

*They'll come for us, you know?*

*Why will they come for us?*

*We must have left evidence there.*

*We picked up all the bits of the brick. We even took pieces out of the mess that used to be his head.*

*We think you thought of everything.*

*We did think of everything. Clothes, shoes, gloves. All taken care of. They're not coming for us.*

*They'll make links between us and him.*

*But they won't make links between us and the others. They're looking for a serial killer. We're not a serial killer. We just wanted him out of our life.*

*Well that's happened. Why haven't we disposed of the knife?*

*We can't stop now.*

*We can't? Why not?*

*If we stop, they'll ask why. They'll realise he was the target after all. We have to keep the murders going to throw them off the scent.*

*Are you crazy?*

*It seems logical to us. Who can we target next?*

I made myself comfortable on my bed, sharpened my knife, and gave it some thought.

# SCRATCHING IN THE DUST

I slipped sideways on a loose pile of iron shavings and concrete shale as I crested the final mountain of debris, jarring my knee. Sucking in my breath in annoyance, I paused to stretch my leg out and catch my breath. Ahead of me lay the market—what remained of it—and beyond that the grey rubble of the ruined city sprawled in every direction.

I wheezed and hacked and coughed up a wad of thick infected phlegm, spitting it to the side of me with a grimace. The dust was ubiquitous, and it was ruining my lungs. I suppose I'd been one of the lucky ones though—at least I remained alive. These days, everyone's life expectancy had been severely curtailed. Most of us would be lucky to make it past forty. I had eight years maybe.

Twenty years after The War, and over eighty per cent of the population had perished. The maternity rate continued to be negligible. We humans were a dying breed. It had been the poisoning of the water after the initial onslaught of bombs that had been the final straw. Everyone needs water to survive—regardless of the make of car they once drove, how many mistresses they had kept, or how deep the bunker they had dug.

I didn't want to stay up here for too long. The stench of rotting flesh had dissipated years ago, corpses and carcasses had been picked clear by carrion, but occasionally, the putrefaction of something long buried far among the shifting rubble beneath my feet inveigled its way through air pockets and made me gag. I hefted my rucksack and carefully started to slip and slide my way down into the dip, the location for the daily market.

I'd had a good day at Gulliver's, where I was employed. All the new industry took place outside the city now, in abandoned factories and warehouses. I worked as a 'cleaner'. Not that anything was clean, or even a close approximation. I suppose a better term for the job I did was a dismantler. The foragers brought in mechanical items, or anything that could be stripped down, and my job involved carefully taking things apart and filing each component, no matter how tiny, into the correct storage bin to be sold on to our Overseers and their team of engineers. I'd dismantled a vacuum cleaner and a hairdryer this morning, and an old-fashioned radio this afternoon. I preferred the really antique stuff, the parts were complicated and intricate. It made the job more interesting, albeit fiddly, whereas twenty-first century hair dryers were simply constructed from plastic. Nobody wanted or needed plastic anymore. The damn stuff was everywhere.

My boots scrunched on the ground as I headed into the market. It was a covered area, dulled plastic sheeting had been roughly tied over scaffolding, and warped wood had been laid out to serve as counter tops for the twenty or so stalls here. Merchandise was minimal though, and what there was of it was limp and grey, coated with dirt. As we all were. This was the state of the world we inhabited.

I kept my chin down and eyes on the floor to avoid the looks of resignation, boredom, or pure desperation from the traders I didn't frequent. The market wasn't busy, so I had little opportunity of blending into obscurity, and while none of them were looking at me, I knew they all saw me. I headed straight for Joanne, as usual, an old acquaintance, she would treat me well.

"Lucie," she greeted me. "Good day?"

I nodded shyly, then lifted my hand and uncurled my fingers. A number of old coins nestled dully on my filth-encrusted palm.

"Not bad," Joanne agreed, and her lips curled slightly.

"I have this too." I offered her my other hand. "I snuck it out." She reached for what I held, but I pulled my hand back in alarm. She jumped. "Sorry. Sorry," I said in a rush. "Be careful. It can bite you."

Puzzled, she indicated that I should place the item on the counter. I did so: a thin sliver of wood and a couple of pieces of metal.

"What is it?"

"Gulliver told me it's a mousetrap. It's spring loaded. Look," I demonstrated how to pull the lever back. "You load food here. The mouse tries to eat it. The pressure of him doing so makes the trap slam shut, and he can't get out. See?"

Joanne laughed in delight. "Ain't that quaint?"

"A forager found a whole box of them somewhere and brought them in. I swiped this one. You want it?"

Joanne shrugged, but I could tell by the twinkle in her eye she did. I didn't. I happily traded to give the awful contraption a new home.

"I could use it, I guess. Beats laying poison everywhere, don't it?"

I nodded and looked at what she had on display, a pitiful collection of odds and sods. Joanne hastily picked up a few potatoes and a turnip. "I got these," she said, "and there's these lentils. You like lentils. And here, you can have a few twists." Joanne twisted salt, pepper and any other herbs she could get her hands on into tiny packages. They were a godsend, really helped to flavour the mundane day-to-day vegetables and bland rat meat we had to survive on.

I accepted what she offered. I wasn't unhappy with the trade, given so little choice. I packed the goods away in my rucksack. Joanne watched me. I started to walk away, when she stopped me.

"Wait," she said in a low voice. "Have this. Put it away, quick." She passed me a small round tin, cool to the touch. Hurriedly I stuffed it in my pocket and scuffled away. If she didn't want anyone else to see what she had given me, I wouldn't betray her confidence. Not so long ago, before The Organization took charge, people were killed for morsels of food. I remembered those days and remained watchful at all times.

I trudged homewards on what passed as a road. The rubble from office blocks and shops—destroyed during The War—towered above me on both sides, towers of concrete, twisted metal, and rusting iron that blocked half-demolished buildings from my view. The foragers occasionally picked through the piles here, and although less and less was of any use to us, I still found the occasional treasure: twisted teaspoons or bicycle wheels with rusted spokes, so I scanned the ground as well as the horizon.

A quick small movement down one of the intermittent alleyways drew my attention. I wouldn't normally have dared to look, but whatever had caught my eye moved low to the ground. I paused and peered into the shadows. The thing moved again, watched me watching it. A dog.

I tutted and moved on. Dogs were rare these days. Straight after The War they had roamed the streets in huge numbers, but they—like everything else—needed water to survive. Dogs and humans alike had been poisoned or gone mad with thirst. Those canines that had managed to survive had been hunted down and used as meat, until the farms had been established way out of town beyond Gulliver's. Maybe dogs were making a comeback. I didn't care. I continued my walk home.

The dog followed me. I studiously ignored it. It would be seen and that would be the end of it. It would be someone's dinner.

A quarter of a mile farther on, I ducked down another alley and followed a twisting path through the rubble. Beneath the overhang of a ruined Victorian hotel, I found the dwelling I called home. I pushed the door and peered in cautiously. Little point in locking up when I left, I had nothing worth stealing.

I dropped my rucksack and turned to push the door closed. The dog stood on the front step watching me. I scowled.

"Go away," I said, and then felt cross that I'd connected with the damn thing. It tilted its head and stared at me with soft brown eyes.

"No." I shook my head. "I have nothing to give you. And I don't need you here."

The dog stood and padded into my room, climbed onto my bed and curled up there. I watched in disbelief.

"Are you kidding me? Get off there. You're filthy."

But that was a lie. The dog was relatively clean. I could see his brown and white coat clearly. He was cleaner than the faded throw that covered my bed.

Puzzled, I approached him and put my hand out tentatively. The dog didn't move. I held my breath and touched him. His fur was soft, a little gritty, but otherwise clean. He smelled fresh. He'd had a bath recently. Where had he found enough water for a bath? Or who had given him one?

I grunted and turned away. I needed to eat. I started a small fire in my fire pit and poured some of my own precious, rationed water into a pan, rubbed the worst of the dirt off the potatoes and turnip with a rag, then cut them up into small chunks and dropped them into the water to parboil them. While I waited, I swept my little home, as though that would make much difference, and carefully rearranged the small collection of trinkets and treasures I had scavenged: a Barbie doll, a plastic train, a few books. It was my one connection to my old life, before The War, when I had been a child.

Only twelve when The War came, everyone I knew died—my parents, my little brother, my friends. I sought shelter with other survivors, and I'd been lucky. There had been lawlessness of course. People were traumatized by so much death. But I survived, thanks to the kindness of strangers, my biddableness, my instincts, my ability to pick out good people—like Joanne—and by keeping my head down.

When the potatoes and turnip softened, I threw them in a frying pan to finish them off. Remembering the tin Joanne had given me, I picked it out of my pocket. It had no label. It would be pot luck then. I located a rusted tin opener among my treasures and with some difficulty peeled back the lid. It was fish of some kind. Tuna probably. It had been a long time since I'd eaten fish. I added it to the frying pan. Tonight I'd enjoy a proper feast.

I ate out of the pan using a spoon. It was good. Different. The dog eyed me, patiently waiting for me to finish. I didn't save him any. I didn't want to encourage him to stay. But as I stood to scour the pan clean with some sand, I relented and set the pan on the floor so that he could lick my leavings.

"You have to go," I said as he finished. I opened the door. He trotted out obediently, then looked back at me. I closed the door on his gaze.

*** 

The following evening, he was waiting for me as I left the market. Once again he had been hiding in the alley. I didn't know whether to feel exasperated or pleased. I decided on the former and walked on. The dog yipped quietly behind me. I stopped and turned back. It had never made a sound the previous day. Drawing attention to itself was a dangerous thing for it to do, but I didn't expect it to understand that.

The dog and I regarded each other and then it ran back down the alley. Hesitating, I decided to follow it, at least for a way. I scrambled down the rubble into the alley, my boots slipping on loose chunks of concrete and shale. The dog trotted to a door cast in shadow at the rear of the alley, and I quickly caught up with it.

I stood and gaped. In front of me was a green wooden door, the paint fresh and bright. I reached out, my dirty fingers caressed the sheen of the paint, expecting it to be wet. It was dry, and looking closely I could see a thin layer of dust covering the door. It had been freshly painted recently. I wondered who would live here and why they would bother to paint a door that would be grey within days.

The dog whined beside me and sat, looking up at me expectantly. It wanted me to go in.

"No," I said, imagining someone on the other side armed with a machete or similar weapon. The dog whined again. He was placing me in a quandary. What if his owner had been hurt and needed help? I should help if I could.

I tapped nervously on the door. There was no response. I tapped harder. Again nothing. The third time I rapped noisily, but no-one came. I huffed my cheeks and considered. The dog scratched the door. There was nothing for it. I turned the antiquated knob. The door opened easily, swung inwards with a satisfying whoosh. I stepped forwards into a small bare room, containing a mop and bucket, a broom cupboard, and some wellington boots. It was clean. I could smell the soap. I inhaled deeply. Cleanliness was the headiest of all perfumes.

The dog trotted happily in beside me and walked straight to the cupboard. With nothing to lose, I pulled that door open too.

And gasped in shock.

It wasn't a cupboard at all, but an opening into a dream, or something half remembered. Outside—behind me—the world was rubble and grit, grey dust accompanied by the putrid stench of decay. But here, inside, colour lit up the world in every shade, the cheerful chirruping sounds of contented birds and the sweetest and lightest of scents drifting towards me on the breeze. Heaven blossomed in a garden such as I'd never imagined.

I stepped forwards into paradise. My heavy boots sank into spongey earth, and when I looked down, I marvelled at their clunky ugliness, compared to the delicate daisies of a neatly groomed lawn.

"You can take them off," a young voice nearby suggested.

Startled, I clenched my fists and whirled around.

"Sorry, I didn't mean to frighten you. Only, if you want to, you can take them off." A young boy of about eight or nine years jumped from a wall to the right of me and landed softly on the grass.

"Who are you?" I demanded. He seemed oddly familiar, but I couldn't quite place him. I knew most of the survivors in the vicinity, as well as their families.

"I'm Derek. You're Lucie."

Puzzled, I stared at the boy. He wore knee-length blue shorts and a t-shirt with some cartoon character emblazoned across the chest. His knees and cheeks were smeared with mud, and his clothes had grass stains. But his dirt was clean and fresh. It wasn't ingrained through years of toil in the acrid city beyond.

Derek. The name rang a bell. And he knew my name too.

"Where are your people?" I asked. I couldn't see anyone else around. Just us and the dog.

He shrugged. "They come and they go. Thank you for bringing Bailey back. He runs off."

"I had a dog called Bailey once," I said. The words came out of me in a rush. Memories that tasted warm and loving. I bit them back. No point in remembering what happened before. "You shouldn't let him run off," I said coldly. "What are you doing here, anyway?" I gazed around, deeply impressed by the quality of the soil here—everything so abundant. The farmers would love this place. I thought of the superiority of the goods they could produce. I wondered why they didn't know about it.

Derek shrugged. "Playing," he said.

Playing. Such a simple concept, but I was awed into a stunned silence. No-one played any more. Perhaps cards to while away the late evening, but mostly we all worked, and then we ate, and then we slept. We didn't do any of that particularly well. But that's what we did, that's what it meant to survive in this place.

"Would you like to play?" Derek asked plaintively. "I haven't had anyone to play with for a long time." He skipped away from me, followed a winding path down the bank, Bailey trotting nonchalantly at his heels. I followed.

The garden was huge. As a child, my family had visited a stately home and I had romped in the garden there. Like that one, this space had been divided into sections: an enormous lawn, glades, a meticulously laid out kitchen garden, and most incredible of all, a small maze. But the sight that stopped me in my tracks was a small lake, surrounded by reeds and tall flowers, their heads drooping lazily as they studied their own reflections in the clear water.

And yes, the water *was* clear. The sun reflected off the surface, and I fancied I could see the sandy bottom. Minnows darted here and there, gliding this way, then shooting off quickly in the opposite direction. I edged closer and reached out to dip my hand in, but instinct held me back.

"Is the water poisoned?"

"Poisoned?" Derek frowned.

I folded my arms, tucking my hands out of sight, away from temptation. The water could be pure acid for all I knew. Perhaps the minnows were an adapted species.

"It's not poisoned," Derek said and plunged his hand in up to the wrist, agitating the water and surprising a number of spectacular blue dragon flies. I backed away, fearful of being splashed by the toxic water. Derek watched me. I could see from the wary look that drifted across his face, he thought me odd.

But he was a child and artless. "Would you like an apple?" he cried. "Look, the ones over here are ready to drop. Come on!" He raced away. After a second I followed him, lumbering clumsily in my great boots, as he dashed sprite-like ahead of me.

The apple tree was huge and old, gnarled and twisted. Branches bowed under the weight of the heavy, ripe fruit. Derek reached up and pulled at an apple and then threw it my way. I lunged for it awkwardly and missed. It fell on the grass with a thump. I scooped it up quickly and stared at it in astonishment. It was firm in my grasp, hardly marked at all. I lifted it to my face and sniffed. The light, delicately perfumed fragrance made my mouth water.

I dropped my hand. "I can't." Everyone knew the only food safe to eat should be grown in the sterile environment of the undercover farms beyond Gulliver's. It was foolhardy to eat anything that had been exposed to the radiation in the atmosphere.

"Don't you like apples?" asked Derek and pulled one off the branch for himself. He opened his mouth and bit deeply into the shiny skin. I drew my breath in sharply. Derek stared at me as he chewed. "It's good," he said, his mouth full of creamy flesh.

I turned the apple over in my hand. I wanted to taste it. How I wanted to.

I gaped at Derek as he munched noisily. Then I lifted my hand and brought the apple to my lips. It was smooth. I caressed the skin with my tongue, so fresh, and then opened my mouth wide. It took more effort than I remembered. I bit into it, the sweetness exploding in my mouth, the crunch reverberating in my ears. I sucked on the juices, chewed, waited for something bitter to replace the taste sensation, but nothing did and so I swallowed. I finished the apple in thirty seconds flat, and Derek handed me another one with a smile.

"You must be hungry!" He laughed in delight. I found myself smiling back at him.

After that, I toured the garden in Derek's wake. He

showed me raspberries and tomatoes, green beans and pots full of herbs. Fascinated by them all, I sniffed them, tasted them, turned my nose up at the sharpness of the raspberries but ate my fill of tiny tomatoes, sweet and red and firm.

"Who looks after all of this?" I asked the boy.

Derek considered the question with all of the gravity he possessed, but the question flummoxed him. "I don't know," he said. "Maybe we all do."

*** 

Maybe we do.

We don't, but maybe we can do, I thought later. I had returned home as the light began to fail, aware of the curfew and tired from all the fresh air. I didn't understand how the garden had not been discovered by the foragers, and I couldn't get my head around the fact that such a glorious place existed. Derek had elicited from me a promise that I would return, and I intended to.

The next day at Gulliver's, my fingers resumed scrabbling among the muck and scratching in the dust as was customary. As I unfastened bolts and prized joints apart, I detected a sense of urgency and excitement in my movements. For once, I had something to look forward to at the end of the day.

I had no intention of spilling the secret about the garden. Its mere existence filled me with joy and hope, two emotions I hadn't experienced at all during the past twenty years. I practically bounced with excitement when Gulliver finally let her workers go. We filtered off in every direction. I walked the two miles back into the city, climbing the mountains of debris—small lumps of concrete skittering in all directions—with a renewed vigour, anxious in case the garden had been a dream and didn't actually exist at all.

But there it was, through the green door still bright and shiny, and then through the cupboard door, mundane in the extreme. The sun shone on my face as I moved out of the shadows. It warmed me. Greeting Derek and Bailey, I divested myself of my boots; painfully peeled three layers of socks away from my stinking, wrinkled feet; and stood barefoot on grass for the first time in two decades. Derek stared down in barely concealed disgust at the grey flesh of my feet and my curled yellow toenails. He shot off in the direction of the lake.

Stems of grass tickled the arches of my feet and wormed their way between my toes. It felt extraordinary. I hadn't realized how much my feet ached until I experienced the coolness of the earth against my skin. It seemed to draw the pain from my muscles. It was agonizing but sensational at the same time.

I hobbled after Derek, both afraid and exhilarated as I drew closer to the water. Derek had perched on the edge, sitting on the grass. He patted a rock, and I sat down, awkwardly, next to him.

"What's wrong with your feet?"

"I haven't bathed them much," I said, meaning not at all. Not since I'd been a kid.

"Is the rest of you like that?"

"No," I smiled at his temerity. "Not so bad, I think."

"You should get in the water."

"I can't swim."

"Just put your feet in then. It won't hurt. I do it all the time. Look." He slipped his shoes off and jumped into the lake. I watched him, recoiling from the splashing.

"Why are you so scared?" he asked. The disdain in his voice hurt a little. I didn't have many friends. Didn't want them. Derek was just a little boy, but I wanted him to like me. That was dangerous for me. I couldn't risk becoming emotionally entangled with anyone, even a kid.

I stood abruptly. "Let's get some apples," I shouted and ran for the tree, forgetting the pain in my feet momentarily. I heard Derek laugh and then he ran too, overtaking me with ease. I thundered after him, my breath wheezing in and out of my ruined lungs. I halted at the tree, bent over, coughed and coughed as phlegm worked its way up and out of me—infected and bloody. I hawked into the long grass, trying to avoid Derek seeing. When I had myself under control, I turned back to him. He held out an apple.

"They say an apple a day keeps the doctor away," he offered, and I nodded, my eyes prickling with unshed tears. The old sayings. Things my mother would say. I shook the memories away.

"Where are your parents?" I asked.

Derek didn't answer, just chewed on his apple. I bit into mine, enjoyed the tangy, crisp sweetness, glad when it washed away the metallic taste of blood from my mouth.

"Let's play on the swings!" demanded Derek and away he ran again, Bailey barking and leaping at him as he went. I plucked another few apples from the tree and followed at a more sedate pace.

The play area was wild with dog daisies and yellow wort, nodding their heads in the tall grass. Butterflies danced from flower to flower, and bees buzzed lazily among them. I couldn't recall seeing butterflies and bees for many years, but here they were thriving. A neat path had been mown through the grass, and a pair of swings hung on chains from a tall metal skeleton, freshly painted the same shade of bright green as the front door.

"Someone does look after this place," I said, more to myself than to Derek who didn't seem to care. He had climbed up onto one of the wooden seats and was already pushing himself backwards and forwards.

"Come on!" he shouted. "Let's fly!"

And I did. Tentatively at first. I let my feet do the work, before my stomach muscles—unaccustomed to the action of pushing—instinctively took over. I settled into the rhythm, drawing back and then flowing forwards. Higher I flew, the blood rushing through my veins in exhilaration. Backwards and forwards, to and fro, higher and higher. I soared through the air, free like a bird, and all I saw was the garden ... fresh and green and alive all around me. No dust, no dirt, no debris.

But suddenly it felt alien and wrong. I slammed my bare feet painfully into the ground, slid to a stop and flung myself from the swing. The momentum catapulted me into the long grass where I retched uncontrollably, the apple I'd eaten quickly regurgitated, and then I started dry heaving.

I felt a small hand on the centre of my back. "Are you okay?" Derek's concerned voice came from far away.

How could I tell him of my fears? How afraid, how desperately frightened I felt. Not of the water or the apples or the swings. But because these things didn't exist in my world I found it easier to live without them than to know of them, to experience them, and to fall in love with them, and have them cruelly taken away. Everything I had loved in my life had been stolen violently away at some stage or another, when I was young. I'd adapted and survived. I didn't want hope or beauty in my life, only for it to be snatched away again.

What if somebody else had followed me here? What if someone stumbled across the door? What would The

Organization think of this place? What would they do to it? They would turn it into a farm, try to feed everyone. It would become contaminated, and it would fail. It would die. I couldn't bear it.

Derek's hand pressed firmly on my back. I shrugged him off, pushed myself to standing and walked away. Away from the swings, past the maze and the apple trees, past the raspberry bushes, the vine tomatoes and the lake. Dragon flies hovered curiously in front of my face, keeping a perfect distance, and then zipped off. Derek called to me. I didn't look back, simply collected my heap of socks and my boots and strolled on.

Stony faced, I pulled the green door firmly shut. Behind me was sunshine, in front of me, only shadow. I turned for home and walked barefoot among the rubble of a ruined civilization.

\*\*\*

"You're pretty sick," Joanne said to me one evening months later as the sun dropped steadily to the horizon and I wheezed my way up to her sparse stall.

"I'm all right."

We all got sick. Joanne wasn't immune. She and I were more or less the same age, but if I looked as old and worn out as she did at this relatively young age, I knew my time was limited. I handed over my day's takings, and she passed me a pile of dried out root vegetables and three tiny green tomatoes, too soft now to ever ripen. I gawped at them, remembered the sweet tomatoes, as red as blood, I'd eaten in the garden.

"New from the farm. You could probably do with a fair few of these to get some vitamins inside you." I shrugged. No chance of that. No point in speaking of it. I turned to leave, but Joanne stopped me. "I heard that someone caught a dog or something. They're cooking it in the square now. Maybe you could get some? Meat would do you good." She offered me some of my coins back.

My stomach rolled, and I looked at Joanne in mute shock. It was the kind of news I'd dreaded since I'd discovered the garden. What if the dog in question was Bailey? I wheeled around and stumbled out of the market.

In order to get home I had to pass right through the square where a small crowd were gathering around a fire pit. I could smell roasting flesh, so held my breath and averted my eyes, not wanting to see the small animal strung up on the spit, being turned slowly as onlookers drooled in anticipation. I walked away rapidly, the vegetables tumbling from my grasp as I went, the tomatoes exploding when they hit the floor.

What a waste. Such a waste. I felt heartily tired of it. The death, the destruction, the futility of picking out a life in the rubble and the dust. I stepped up the pace to get away from the stink of the dog on the spit, but my lungs burned with the effort of trying to walk through the loose concrete chippings too quickly, and I slowed down in order to prevent a painful coughing fit that would see me leave half a lung in the gutter.

I drew level with the alley where I had first seen Bailey and reluctantly looked for him. I could see no discernible movement through the twilight gloom. Casting a wary eye around me, I picked my way through the alley, under the overhang, through to the dead end. No sign of the dog. I would have liked to pretend that I had never thought of him, or of Derek, in the intervening months since I'd walked out of the garden, but that would have been a lie. I didn't dwell on them, because that would be too painful, but I carried them in my memory and in my heart. Something I had never intended to do. Thinking of them, took me home. Back to the past. Back when I had a family. I missed them. I missed them all.

I paused in front of the door. The bright green paint had faded to grey now, lost under dense layers of dust and filth. I scraped some away with my finger, exposed the colour. Wrote my name, Lucie, considered it my epitaph, and turned the handle. The store room seemed much as it had been before, just a little mustier, the faint scent of detergent masking something old and long forgotten.

I caught my breath and reached out for the handle of the cupboard door. It felt cold in my grip. What would I see beyond? I feared it would be an extension of the world I had left behind me and not the garden I remembered. I held the door, inching it forward, then let it spring fully open. I was momentarily blinded by bright midday sunshine. It was always daytime here.

I stepped out onto the grass, the earth spongy beneath my feet and damp with recent rainfall, the trees bowing under their sodden foliage. The air smelled fresh and clean. Relieved, I breathed deeply, without setting off my cough. Somewhere ahead of me I heard a child laughing. Derek. And the answering bark of a dog. My spirits lifted. All was well, then. We could be together.

I wanted to feel clean inside and out. I wanted to divest myself of fear. I headed for the lake, and there at the edge I impatiently unlaced my boots and threw them into the water. The water didn't bubble and froth and dissolve them, the boots simply bobbed for a moment and sank out of sight.

I ripped the clothes from my body. Layer after layer. Rag after rag. Methodically at first, desperately at the end.

My pale grey flesh disgusted me—thin and unwholesome and difficult to look at—but I was determined now not to hide from my own gaze. Not my memories, not my fears, not my hopes, and certainly not my physical reality.

Naked, I plunged waist deep into the lake. I expected to be burned by the water, but instead found myself stunned and exhilarated by the sharp coldness of it. Shivering, I walked farther in until the water lapped at my breasts.

I heard Derek calling my name joyfully, and I smiled. It filled my heart with an unknown warmth to hear his pleasure. How good it is to love and be loved. I dropped backwards, lifted my feet, let the water carry me, surround me. I lay my head back, and the water pulled me down. Eyes open, I studied my surroundings, watched the minnows dash this way and that among the reeds. I sank lower, breathed out, watched the bubbles escaping, heading for the sunshine at the surface.

And breathed in.

# IN KINDNESS

With weary resignation I joined the throng of people shuffling into the station while surreptitiously attempting to hike my underwear up underneath my skirt. The elastic in my pants was a little worn, and both they and my tights were heading south alarmingly quickly. I glanced around, recognising that the fiddling with my undergarments was bound to be recorded on CCTV somewhere.

I scowled. I was hot, sweaty, and completely fed up. It was Friday afternoon rush hour in Central London and an unseasonably warm day. Too warm. I had had no desire to even visit London—a city deluded by its own bloody self-importance. My manager had decreed I spend the best part of the working day in a meeting with a client, at the client's convenience rather than mine. That was fine as far as it went, but I had expected to finish at three, allowing me plenty of time to travel to Paddington and catch my train back to Exeter. I'd be home reasonably early and able to enjoy my weekend.

That had been the plan. The meeting had overrun. Of course it had. These male bigwigs, they like the sound of their own voices and relish the power they have of dictating what the rest of us do, how and when. The client droned on and on and on. He had nothing new or interesting to say after the first thirty minutes, and yet all day I remained awkwardly seated, looking slightly to my left at him, therefore ending up with a crick in the neck. All the while I nodded, smiled, appearing intelligent and interested, resisting the urge to yawn, to allow my eyes to glaze over, or to start dribbling into my coffee.

Speaking of coffee, I had definitely consumed too much. And eaten too many biscuits. The waist band of my skirt felt tight, I badly needed to pee, and damn it, there went my tights again.

I paused at the top of the steps to try and pull everything back into place. An old woman heading laboriously up the stairs caught my eye and smiled. She was wearing a bright yellow scarf. Canary yellow. It was the perfect colour for a spring day, and for a moment I was mesmerised by her. She was carrying a number of old plastic bags, stuffed full of belongings, and a large wicker basket containing packages. She was small and slight, but thanks to her bags, she was taking up a fair amount of space. People rushed past her, oblivious to her load.

I was in the way. Behind me some ignoramus tutted loudly, then swore and jolted past me, knocking my arm as he went. My fingers snagged in my waist band and ripped the nail from my middle finger.

"Oh for fuck's sake!" I said a little too loudly. Some woman heading up into the open air gave me a disapproving look. What? Like she'd never cursed in her life?

The idiot who had purposefully bumped into me steamed down towards the underground passage. Obviously in a bit of a rush, he didn't care who he bulldozed out of his way. I started down the stairs after him and watched helplessly as he ploughed into the woman with the canary yellow scarf.

In the immediate aftermath of the collision, the woman hung in time, briefly suspended in mid-air, but she had been knocked off balance and inevitably she began to fall backwards. Open-mouthed, I lunged for her, watching as she let go of her basket. I couldn't get past the people in front of me though, and I couldn't have reached her in time. She toppled backwards, slid down the steps, and landed on her bottom, in an undignified heap of skirts and coat and bags and packages.

The woman howled in anger. Two people stopped to help but recoiled from her ferocity and quickly hurried away. Other people side-stepped her and her packages. Everyone else ignored her. I was gobsmacked. Everyone in London was so damn busy and selfish they couldn't stop to help another human being? Seriously?

I reached the bottom of the stairs, picking up packages as I went. The first thing that hit me was her stench. She stank. Unclean. Old dried urine. And worse. I tried not to breathe it in.

"Are you all right, love?" I asked, straightening her basket and popping her packages back inside.

Her wide and wandering eyes were a startling pale green, her face old and lined, grey with tiredness. "My things..." she beseeched me, her voice cracked with age.

I nodded. Her plastic bags had not fallen far. From what I could see they contained clothes and newspapers, some photos, and tins of food. The paper packages from the basket had scattered a little further afield. I couldn't tell what was in them. People bustled around me as I fumbled on the floor, trying to collect everything.

I returned everything and knelt next to her. Her chin was on her chest, her stringy hair flat against her skull. "Are you hurt?" I asked. "Or do you think you can stand up?"

She sighed theatrically and nodded, and so I put one hand under her left armpit and the other around her right elbow and hoisted her to her feet. She was as light as a feather. Her bulk was caused by the layers of clothes she was wearing. She might as well have been stuffed with goose down.

She cooed as I slackened my grip. I was dimly aware that I was going to miss yet another train to Exeter but I couldn't leave her at the bottom of the steps, not with the crush of people advancing on us.

"Let me help you to the top of the stairs," I said, perhaps hoping that she would protest that I had done enough or something similar, but she didn't. She merely held her basket out to me. I took it—along with her plastic bags—while she tucked her arm through mine and with her free hand held on to the railing as we climbed the steps slowly, slowly, until we were back out in the early evening sunshine.

Once we were at the top I handed the basket over. "Will you be ok now?" I asked.

She offered a half smile. It was all I could do not to look away in disgust. Her teeth were black and yellow, her lips dry and cracked. She flicked her tongue over her lips and for a fleeting moment I saw an unusually pointed tongue, crusted a thick, furry green.

Startled, I blinked.

When I looked again, she'd closed her mouth.

She rummaged in the basket among the packages, weighing each one in her hand and considering it. She settled on one which she handed to me.

I started to protest but she dismissed me with a wave of her hand. "You're kind," she croaked. "It's important to be kind." Before I could respond she had spun around and walked quickly away. She was suddenly incredibly agile for an old woman who had fallen down the stairs. I watched her go, puzzled, and then, tucking the package into my bag with one hand while fiddling with my pants and tights with the other, I raced for my train.

*** 

By some miracle I made it. The train was slightly delayed and the gates were closing as I shot through them. I threw myself through the first set of doors and heard the imperious whistle from the guard. The train lurched, and we were off. My heart hammered with exertion, my breath ragged and uneven.

The train was crammed. There were students sitting on their rucksacks outside the toilets. Looking into the carriages I could see men in business suits with their newspapers and iPads, neat young women with their Kindles and mobile phones, and a variety of Asian tourists with maps and bags of food.

As the train left the station I urged one of the students to move, and popped into the loo. It was such a relief to be able to pull my damn tights down and release my bladder. I thanked the gods heartily for smelly train toilet cubicles.

Done, I tidied myself up. I was a revolting combination of sweaty and dusty. My hair was beyond redemption and my face an unappealing shade of salmon pink, but finally, collected enough to pass muster with the general public, I exited the cubicle and stepped over the students once more to begin the hunt for a seat as the train picked up speed and rocked a little over the rails.

With difficulty, I fought through a number of carriages, each equally as packed as the one before it. I was beginning to give up hope and resign myself to standing, at least as far as Reading, when something blew across my field of vision. A feather fluttered down from the overhead baggage store. I watched it settle on my right shoulder. It was bright yellow. I brushed it off, and it flew gracefully through the air and landed on a vacant window seat. I'd assumed the seat was taken because it was covered by a bag and a coat.

Smiling as pleasantly as I could I leaned down to the gentleman in the aisle seat. "Is that one taken?"

The slightly overweight chap—dressed in the requisite business suit with tie at half-mast and clutching a can of cheap lager, signalling the weekend was indeed upon us— looked up at me and grunted. I widened my smile further, resisting the urge to sarcastically enquire whether his bag had paid for its seat. After an eternity he stood up and stowed his belongings overhead. I slid in and settled next to the window.

Finally, I could relax.

I let my mind wander freely. The outskirts of London passed smoothly by. I was entranced by the large Victorian buildings and imagined the landscape hadn't changed much over the past century. What ghosts inhabited the old buildings and churches? What stories could the old factories tell? I fell into a reverie for a while, lulled by the gentle movement of the train, the warmth of the day, and my own tiredness.

The buffet cart rattled into the carriage, jerking me back to consciousness. "Anything from the bar for you? Cold drinks? Snacks?" chimed a voice.

I riffled through my handbag to locate my purse, but found the package the old woman had given me instead. Wrapped neatly in white paper, it was about the size of a pair of socks and probably weighed the same.

"Anything from the bar for you?" The young woman was addressing the man sat next to me now. I hastily returned the package to my bag, found my purse, and ordered a double gin and tonic and a bottle of water. I downed the water in one and then started on the gin and tonic. With no delays we could expect to arrive into Exeter at around eight-ish. Alleluia.

I settled back again, nonchalantly scanning my fellow travellers. The guy opposite was an older man. He looked distinguished, clean-cut and handsome, but his white shirt had a brown stain above the nipple which I found rather disconcerting.

With a flash of recognition, I realised that the man next to him was my adversary from the Paddington entrance. He was the one who had knocked the woman down the steps. I stared at him. For all his rushing, where had it got him? He was still on the same train as me. He was young, early twenties, but his suit suggested he was paid well and thought he was going places. I glowered at him. He turned to look at me quizzically. I gave him my best hard glare and pointedly turned to look out of the window, well aware of how ridiculously passive aggressive I was being. I didn't give a flying fart.

\*\*\*

Thirty minutes later it was beginning to get dark and I needed to pee again. The G and T had worked its way through nicely.

Magic.

I excused myself to my chunky seat mate, who took it as a personal affront that I had to make him move once more, and headed for the toilet.

As I washed my hands, I peered in the mirror. I looked tired. It had been a long day. I leaned closer to better examine the wrinkles around my eyes.

The lights went off.

My breath caught in my throat in surprise. I automatically put my hands out to steady myself, laying them flat against the wall in front of me, but it was so dark I could hardly see them at all. My face was still just inches from the mirror.

Shadows crossed in front of me. I looked for my reflection. Curious eyes narrowed in a frown. Were they mine? I peered into the blackness, saw a tiny speck of light... no, two little pins of light... coming closer, getting larger. I leaned in, and suddenly a face leapt out of the mirror at me. It was human of sorts. Its eyes were a murky mustard yellow, its nose a snout above lips that rolled back, and teeth that snapped and snarled at me.

I shrieked and shot backwards, colliding with the locked door behind me and banging my elbow hard. My feet started to slip on the floor and I stared up at the mirror in fear. The shadows there swirled like a green and golden mist. I recoiled in horror as a hand stretched out towards me, illuminated by a light not of this world. The nails were long and curled; the fingers grimy with muck.

The lock of the door stabbed me in the back. I turned and scrabbled with it. For a moment, in my panic, I couldn't make it work. Sharp nails scratched the fabric of my shirt. Whimpering, I finally managed to slide the lock, fling open the door, and leap into the vestibule.

The train's lights flickered on.

I stood alone in the corridor, my elbow throbbing. The open door of the toilet swung gently in time with the rhythm of the rocking train. I could see my reflection in the mirror, standing open mouthed and pale. The circles beneath my eyes deeper and darker than before.

I took a tentative step forward, inched my way back into the toilet cubicle, and reached out. The glass was cold and hard. My fingertips left smudges. The mirror was a mirror.

Nothing else.

I laughed nervously. What a bloody idiot!

I returned shakily to my seat. It may have been my imagination, but the carriage seemed quieter than before. I smiled at Mr Chunky and squeezed back into my seat. The distinguished chap with the stained shirt who had been sitting opposite me had disappeared, probably to the bar, I decided.

I willed my heart rate to slow down and stared out of the window at the dusk beyond. I wasn't really seeing anything, just concentrating on bringing my breathing under control, but a flickering in the window caught my eye. Someone in the seats on the opposite side of the carriage was standing up. I realised I could see a great deal of the carriage reflected in the window. What a great way to people-watch.

The train headed into a tunnel. The lights in the carriage dimmed, brightened, and then went out again. Someone, somewhere, giggled. Mr Chunky, sitting next to me, swore under his breath. I shifted uneasily in my seat, looking towards the door at the end of the carriage, thinking of the mirror in the toilet. For a moment I could see nothing in the dark, but then, beyond the glass I saw a swirling green mist filling the vestibule like a revolting dry ice. Distinctly lit, it rose from the floor and climbed the walls. I watched as insidious fingers with long muck-encrusted nails curled around the doors, pulling them open. The noxious and poisonous mist spilled into the carriage. People around me coughed and retched.

I sat up straight, alarmed, ready to clamber over Mr Chunky in my efforts to get away from the mist.

The train rushed out of the tunnel with a roar and the lights blinked on again.

111

My adversary, sitting diagonally to me, was smirking. He had obviously smelt my fear in the dark. I scowled at him again and threw myself back in my seat. I had a lot of room. Mr Chunky had disappeared.

Nonplussed I glanced around. The carriage was half empty. How could it be this empty? We hadn't even made it as far as Reading yet. I looked at my watch. We should have passed Reading. Forty minutes from London. I'd been on the train longer than that.

Bewildered, I turned to look out of the window at the passing scenery. Generic but beautiful. British fields and rivers, farms and hamlets. Peaceful, green, and homely. Gorgeously rural. Not unusual enough for me to recall from previous journeys. My stomach churned. Was I on the wrong train?

No, no, I wasn't. I knew I wasn't. What the hell was going on?

I badly wanted to ask him Mr Smug if he had noticed anything odd, or find out where the next stop was, but his curt arrogance, his holier-than-thou attitude, and the image of the old woman falling, falling down the steps at the station prevented me from opening my mouth. I was struck mute in the face of his overwhelming selfishness.

I perched on my seat, my back rigid, my breathing shallow.

My life remained on pause for less than five minutes. With a whooshing sound like an enormous monster breathing in, the train entered another tunnel and the lights went out again. I hooked my fingers claw-like into the arms of the seat and stared once more at the door to the vestibule.

The mist rolled in again, thick and green. Tendrils slunk down the aisle, curled around seat legs, reached up at the shadows occupying those seats. Once again I heard coughing and wheezing. A whimper was abruptly silenced.

This time when the train hurried free of the tunnel and the lights blinked on, I could hardly bear to look up. There were maybe six people left sitting in the carriage.

"Sarah?" I heard a woman call. "Sarah?"

"What the hell?" Finally, Mr Smug was waking up to the fact that something was seriously wrong with this Penzance express. He moved into the aisle to take in his surroundings.

"Where is everyone?"

I started to reply when the train viciously slammed on its brakes.

A woman behind me screamed as we were all flung forwards. Mr Smug was catapulted down the aisle, landing on his backside by the glass door. I was thrown forwards in my chair, my stomach colliding painfully with the table. The train was screaming as the wheels tried to get purchase on the track. Metal ground against metal. The noise filled my head, pulsated through my body, and rang deafeningly in my ears. Then I was thrown backwards as the train finally ground to a halt.

There was silence in the carriage. The few of us left were completely stunned.

I could feel the vibration of the idling engine beneath my feet. Elsewhere there was only silence. Mr Smug clambered to his feet. His face was bleeding. It might have been his chin or his mouth, I couldn't tell.

Three or four voices were babbling behind me. I couldn't understand what they were saying. I stood so that I could join in the general confusion and feel part of it. Safety in numbers. There were three women and two men in the carriage in addition to me and Mr Smug. I began to ask whether everyone was all right, really just to have something to say, when the lights flicked off again.

Someone screamed. I assumed it was the same woman as before. There always has to be a screamer. Someone else moaned.

I remained still. Something brushed against me, something dry and dusty, a long-dead corpse. I shuddered. For a moment the air was fetid, the stench of rotten meat and spoilt milk was overpowering. I gagged and turned my head away, inching away from that putrid stink. I heard a moan come again and then stop. Seconds later the lights were back on, the train was still idling, and I was alone in the carriage with Mr Smug.

In desperation I stumbled into the aisle looking for the others but there was no sign. Luggage nestled in the baggage racks, Kindles and tablets lay on tables and seats—blinking at the ceiling. Handbags had been left un-minded, while newspapers were strewn on tables and abandoned unread. Drinks and sandwiches, mobile phones, and all manner of paraphernalia were strewn across the floor. I hurriedly picked my way through the detritus to the exit at the far end of the carriage and ran across the vestibule to the next carriage. That carriage was empty of people but also full of belongings.

I had an urge to walk the length of the train, but I knew I would find the same thing in every carriage. And if I went to the driver's pod, what then? Would that be empty too? Is that why the train had stopped?

"They can't just have disappeared!" came a voice behind me, loud in my ear. I jumped a mile.

"Jesus! Do you flaming mind? You scared the crap out of me!"

"Touchy, touchy," he muttered. He picked his way back into our carriage, and I followed him. The electric door slid shut behind me with a clank and a hiss.

Then it clicked.

I stopped walking and turned back. It had clicked. I examined the door from a distance. The click had sounded like a lock. There was no obvious evidence that there was a lock on the door. Surely these days the damn things were electronic and controlled by sensors and stuff. Something hi-tech that I didn't understand. I stepped closer to the door. It didn't reopen. I waved at the sensor. Nothing. This door was not going to open.

I ran down the carriage, kicking mobiles and bottles of drink out of my way as I went. Mr Smug cowered away from me as I approached him, perhaps assuming I was going to attack him, but I pushed past him and reached for the door at the opposite end of the carriage. The one I had been using to visit the toilet.

The door opened with a shush as I approached and I slowed, relieved. But just as I reached it, it closed with an angry hiss and again I heard the tell-tale click of a lock.

It was hopeless. My shoulders slumped. I couldn't comprehend what was happening, and I didn't know what to do.

This time when Mr Smug approached me, he cleared his throat. "Both of the doors are locked," I told him. My voice sounded strangely matter of fact.

"They're on sensors," he said, master of the completely bloody obvious. "Here. Mind out."

I stepped out of his way and observed as he stepped towards and away from the door, dancing on the spot and waving at the sensors. Eventually he resorted to brute force by heaving on the door handle, before hammering on the glass with his fists. The doors did not budge.

"The sensors must have failed. The train has failed. That's why the lights keep going off. That's why we've stopped."

"And that's why everyone else has disappeared, is it?" I asked shortly.

He picked up a small rucksack from the table next to him and then put it down again, his face draining of colour.

"They all got off."

"No. They didn't. We haven't stopped anywhere. No-one who joined the train at Paddington has gotten off. Not at a station at any rate."

We studied each other in silence. He looked young now, a small boy, and less the arrogant business graduate or whatever he happened to be.

The lights went out. Flickered on again. Simultaneously, we glanced nervily at the ceiling. I swallowed, my throat dry. The lights were dimming as though the power was draining out of them. We were running out of time.

Behind him, through the glass door I could see the green mist running across the floor, an unholy fog dashing around; tentacles exploring the corners, rivulets chasing after themselves, until they hit an obstacle of some kind—a wall, a door, a rucksack—but they were quick to adapt, to work out that they could climb. Searching for freedom? Searching for victims? Searching for a way to get at us?

What was happening and why had we been saved until last? The fetid mist had rolled past both of us several times. There must have been a reason for that. Was it because we had been sitting centrally in the carriage? Maybe, but the other travellers, including the distinguished gentleman, had been among the first to go.

As I stared at the roiling mist I spotted a heap on the floor. Perhaps someone had dropped their coat. The lighting was weaker, and the shadows growing longer, making it increasingly difficult to see, but I realised I could see the heap of clothes swelling. A small flash of bright yellow among it was growing larger. The mist tumbled and swirled and the heap became a lump, twisting and bubbling among the swirls. The lump grew and grew, the flash of yellow widened. I realised I was watching the unfurling of a body. A small woman with a dark grey coat and a canary yellow scarf.

"Oh my god." I stumbled backwards away from the door towards the middle of the carriage.

Mr Smug followed my gaze, squinted, and then, looking bewildered, he backed away from the door to stand with me.

"This is all about you!" I hissed at him. "What are you on about?"

"That woman!"

"I've never seen her before!"

"You knocked her over at the station. At Paddington. As we were coming down the stairs. You were in such a rush.

You knocked her flying!"

"I don't remember her."

"She was climbing the stairs, coming towards us. She had baskets. You pushed her down."

Mr Smug's mouth dropped open in recognition of what I was saying. He didn't look so smug any more, though.

"She was in my way."

I glared at him. "Are you for real? You knocked an old woman down the stairs! She could have been badly hurt!" "Well, I'm sorry, ok?" Mr Smug was starting to panic.

"I really don't think that's going to cut it," I replied.

The carriage door exploded into a million tiny shards of glass behind him. We both ducked at the sound and shielded ourselves from the flying glass.

Mr Smug hitched his breath in, audibly. Standing at the door was the old woman from the train station, the woman I'd seen in the mirror in the toilets. But she wasn't human. No way. Her eyes glowed in the palest of cold green hues.

Her hair, once greasy and plastered against her skull, swam around her head, long and full, in a luminescent silver halo. Energy poured from every pore of her body, and the air around us fizzed with static. The carriage lights flickered and blinked in response, buzzing noisily.

She advanced into the carriage, jittering and juddering as she came, her movements unearthly and stiff. She didn't walk, but floated three or four inches above the floor, swept in with the green mist that rolled freely from the vestibule. It was uncanny to watch, and my stomach turned in fear and revulsion. The closer she moved towards me, the more nauseous I became. She was old, her skin lined and parchment-dry, with wrinkle forming on wrinkle.

Her eyes sliced through the air around me, looking this way and that, then settled on Mr Smug. I inched backwards as the woman advanced, but my companion seemed locked in place.

"Come on!" I said urgently. "Come away!" But he was paying me no heed.

Frantically, I grabbed his arm. He was a complete idiot, but I couldn't just leave him. I pulled with all my might, but he seemed entirely oblivious to me and only had eyes for the apparition as she drifted towards us.

I moaned in frustration, and the spirit's eyes locked on me briefly. I waved at her, hoping for some recognition. "Hey, hey! It's me! I helped you. Remember?" I could hear the desperate plea in my voice, but she was completely unmoved and after regarding me for one moment longer, turned her attention back to Mr Smug, heading our way faster than before. I didn't want to find out what she was intending to do to us. My mind ran riot with the possibilities. Rip us apart. Eat us. Turn us into the Borg or some wretched idiotic zombies. It would hurt. I was going to die. I had to get out.

I raced back to my seat to search my handbag for something I could use to break the door or a window. Nothing was immediately obvious. I turned it upside down on the table: Used tissues, clean tissues, tampons, book, pens, mints, business cards, a note from my Mum, my mobile, an ancient plastic green top from a packet of *Smarties* I had kept forever, the package the old woman had given me at the station. Nothing useful. Nothing.

I stared down at the table. Watched as the little package twitched just once. Then it began to pulse. I held my breath. The little paper packet was definitely moving—or more correctly, whatever was inside it was. Could this situation get any more bizarre? With shaking hands, I tentatively reached out and touched the package. It was warm and soft.

I snatched up the package. It fitted comfortably in the palm of my hand and wriggled in my grasp. Somewhere in the deep recesses of my mind I understood that whatever this was, it could save the situation. Carefully I tore at the edges of the paper packaging and caught my breath as a tiny feathered head appeared through the hole I had created. It was a bright yellow bird. It twisted and turned and made the hole wider. Then it forced its body out and flew into the carriage, settling on the headrest of a seat in front of me. The package shuddered in my hand and there was another bird working its way out of the hole. And then another. And another.

Dozens of canaries struggled out of the package and found somewhere to settle. The carriage was quickly filled by the twittering of noisy birds. Their chatter grew more and more animated and urgent as increasing numbers of birds sought somewhere to perch. Within a minute of the first bird appearing, there must have been hundreds of its friends jam-packed on every available perch.

And just like that, there was silence. The woman hovered in front of Mr Smug, who was incapable of doing anything to break the spell he was under. The birds watched her carefully, with unblinking, shiny black eyes.

And then one bird—I fancy she was the first one out of the package, but who would know?—started to sing. It was a sweet lyrical song. At first she sang alone, but one by one, the others joined her. The old woman cocked her head and listened to them. The birds sang and sang, initially just a random cacophony of notes, but after a minute or so, I realised there was a great deal of repetition.

The woman nodded in time to the rhythm of the song and held her arms aloft. She swayed and danced, her movements clumsy and rigid. A few of the birds swooped down from their perches to fly around her, and the other canaries sang, faster and faster, encouraging her. Round and round flew the birds, until the old woman was lost from my sight for a moment behind this twisting yellow vortex.

I moved tentatively towards Mr Smug, hoping I could pull him back or wake him up, but as I approached him, the flying birds broke away, and the woman was there, in front of us, close enough for her to touch him. She put one hand up to me in a halting gesture.

My shoulders slumped. I would not be able to help him. "You told me it was important to be kind," I said softly.

I didn't think she would hear me, but she became very still and nodded slowly. For a moment, in my terror, I fancied that her eyes softened a little. A small smile flickered on those dry, cracked lips and she nodded, once. "In kindness," she whispered and then she leant forward, wrapped her arms around Mr Smug, and kissed him full on the lips.

I thought then that it was going to be all right. But certainly her idea of kindness and my idea were at variance. Mr Smug leaned into the kiss for a moment and then he crumpled a little. As I watched in horror, his skin became as pale as paper and he started to lose bulk. The old woman carried on the kiss, and Mr Smug sagged. His legs were paper shells, they no longer had the strength to hold him up. The woman gripped him, her lips elongated, sucking away his life and soul. Within twenty seconds it was all over and she dropped the dry crust that had once been Mr Smug to the floor and stepped back, her face glowing with the brilliance of a supernatural inner light.

She clapped her hands and the birds took flight once more. Fluttering at first, they gained momentum, and faster and faster they circled the carriage. I covered my head with my arms and moved back towards my seat, birds bumping into me and the beating of a thousand tiny wings creating a ferocious draught. I climbed into my seat, drawing my belongings close to me. I hugged my head and slumped forwards against the table. The train lurched, and I cried out in fear. Someone put their hand on my arm; I screamed.

"Sorry," a voice said. Mr Chunky peered down at me, looking slightly embarrassed. "You er... ah ... seem to have been having a bad dream. We've just arrived into Exeter and the train is terminating here."

I sat bolt upright and stared out of the window. We were at Exeter. Lots of people were milling around on the platform outside.

"There's flooding farther down the line at Dawlish, so the train is stopping here."

I looked back at Mr Chunky gormlessly.

"They said there'll be buses." Mr Chunky obviously mistook my silence for dismay at the disturbed travel arrangements.

"No! No! That's great!" I jumped up, hitting my head on the luggage rack. "Thank you, thank you! That's really... kind." I stopped. "To wake me up." I paused. "Thanks."

Mr Chunky nodded, blushed, and made for the carriage door.

He stood behind Mr Distinguished, waiting patiently to leave the train. My head was singing in delight. It didn't happen. It didn't happen. It didn't happen.

I moved into the aisle and packed all my belongings into my handbag. Checking above me, I spotted one long gentleman's coat left on the luggage rack. It could only have been Mr Smug's, although there was no sign of him. I took the coat from its place, noticing his briefcase underneath. The coat unrolled as I dragged it out and I gasped in horrific recognition as I was suddenly showered in        bright        yellow        canary        feathers.

# THE INSTALLATION

The fans were hysterical. Seth loved it that way. The girls at the front of the stage—squashed, sweaty, weeping—turned him on. He grinned out at them as he hung the microphone back on its stand. Dramatically, he ripped his silk shirt off, ran to the edge of the stage and threw it into the mosh pit. Girls opened their mouths to him—wide cavernous Os of ecstasy—screaming themselves hoarse and fighting like piranha fish for a scrap of the expensive purple shirt. The arena stank of sexual possibility. Yes, Seth was aroused.

Behind Seth, the bass player parked his guitar against the amp. Feedback reverberated and shrieked throughout the auditorium, so loud that some members of the audience covered their ears, and the security guys were thankful to be wearing noise dampening earphones. The drummer clambered down from his pedestal and moved with the other members of the band to join Seth at the front. The band looped arms slick with perspiration around each other's necks and took a series of bows. The drummer threw his sticks out into the crowd and these disappeared as speedily as the shirt had done.

With a final wave at the amorphous mass of fans, Seth loped off stage to be handed a towel by a dark-haired girl with crew written on her sweatshirt. He kept walking through to the backstage area where food and drink had been lain out and grabbed a bottle of fizzy water. He couldn't stomach alcohol, and he refused all drugs. He liked his mind clear. Crystal sharp. Backstage, he didn't live up to his hell-raising rock image at all.

He scanned the crowd milling about. His manager routinely brought in 'interesting' people for the group to meet and greet. Many of the girls were barely legal, and they bored Seth rigid. They were clones of each other. All fake tan and skimpy outfits, bouffant hair, too much make-up and iPhones. They had no conversation and fewer ideas. He let the rest of the group take their pick and knew that invariably they would end the night back in a strange and anonymous hotel room with two or three at a time. In the morning the girls would be lucky to get a taxi back to their mothers. They were entirely disposable. Any port in a storm.

No, Seth wanted something entirely different. He looked around again wistfully. His eyes settled on the crew member who had handed him the towel. She was taking a bottle of beer from the table and levering the cap off it using a Swiss Army implement that hung from a chain on her belt. A tall woman of about twenty-four, she had a muscular build especially in the arms and thighs, and large breasts that were settled comfortably on her chest beneath the loose black sweatshirt. She had drawn her long, shining hair back in a tight ponytail. Seth licked his lips. Perfect.

He sidled up to her and smiled. "Hi! I'm Seth."

The woman looked at him and blushed scarlet. Of course she knew who he was; she worked for him. "I'm Cilla," she stammered. "I'm part of the crew."

Seth nodded as though she'd said the most intelligent thing anyone had ever said to him. "Do you enjoy working on the tour?"

"Yes, of course! I've always loved rock music, and I've been a huge fan of this band since I was at school. It's great to be a part of this arena tour. I'm hoping that Jamie will recruit me for the European leg." Cilla indicated the road manager, who had a brittle blonde on each knee, then smiled at Seth.

"Oh I'll have a word with him. I'm sure he will," Seth replied airily. He picked up a couple of bottles of beer and steered Cilla by the arm over to a corner sofa. Cilla blushed again and looked around. No-one paid them any attention so she perched awkwardly on the sofa next to Seth. "Tell me ... what other tours have you done?" he asked her, trying to set her at ease.

For the next ninety minutes or so, Seth listened while Cilla told him how she had taken a degree in Media at University and had then worked for a music magazine for a while before joining a small tour as a roadie. He swapped stories of hedonism and excess from his tours. Cilla listened agog. Seth plied her with bottles of beer, while pretending to drink his, flattering her with references to her practicality and capability.

Cilla started to relax. After a while she shook her long hair out of its pony tail and Seth caught one of the tresses in his hand, commenting on its healthy shine and staring into her brown eyes with his unusually pale blue ones. Cilla was charmed. Seth bent his head and kissed her gently on her mouth, and Cilla's heart exploded in excitement.

The backstage party started to break up. Seth drew away from Cilla and sighed dramatically so that she looked at him with concern. "I hate going back to those anonymous hotels with all these loose girls," he explained, glaring morosely at the bounteous teenagers draped over various band members and management bods. "Look, I don't suppose ..." he pursed his lips and stopped. "No, no. You're far too lovely, I really couldn't impose."

"What?" asked Cilla. "Go ahead, its ok."

Seth shrugged. "I have my car outside. How would you feel about driving back to my house? It's maybe an hour from here. I'd appreciate the company. Nothing untoward. I have loads of ... bedrooms ... you know. We could have toast and marmite."

Cilla laughed at this atypical rock star's peculiar supper penchant. She looked at Seth, pretending to consider this for a moment. Really, there was nothing to contemplate. She nodded. "Okay," she said, "I love marmite."

Cilla couldn't quite believe all that was happening to her in the space of one evening. Realistically, she understood herself to be a plain woman with few opportunities in life and yet here was Seth Blackman, a multi-millionaire rock star, fawning over her and treating her well. For the first time in her short life, Cilla felt glamorous and desirable. Beneath her blushes she secretly relished the poisonous looks the other women sent her way, when she left the venue with Seth holding her hand.

Seth drove a bright red, rock star corvette, flashy and gorgeous. A charming and attentive companion, he unlocked the car and opened the door for Cilla. Her heart pounded when Seth leaned across her to fix her seatbelt. She held her breath as his face brushed her breast. He looked up at her, smiling knowingly, and Cilla tingled. Her nipples hardened under her sweatshirt, and she shifted her weight, feeling her own mounting desire. Her mouth opened involuntarily, and Seth stared at her lips hungrily.

Seth's driving was slick, confident, and sexy—just like him. He had strong hands and muscular forearms. Cilla imagined those on her body, exploring hidden nooks and crannies, and she shivered in anticipation. She lifted her chest and tried to relax.

They drove from London into Surrey at a fast pace. At

this time of night, the roads were quiet and the going was easy. Seth drove steadily down the leafy roads and they continued to chat about pets and books and films. Cilla laughed on cue and tried to seem entertaining and intelligent.

Seth drove up to a pair of large gates and took a remote control from the glove box. The gates slid open, and he manoeuvred through, turning up the winding drive, hung with weeping willows. His huge house, set well back from the road, had a gravel turning space out the front, with mock Grecian pillars for an entrance, and a four-door garage. Seth bounded out of the car and ran to open the door on Cilla's side. He took her arm and walked up to the front door, unlocked it and stood back to let Cilla enter first.

Cilla stood and looked in awe at the huge hallway. The floor was a rather sensational pink marble, and a grand staircase with white carpet and black semi-quavers spiralled away from her, drawing her eye to an enormous chandelier made of Grolsch beer bottles hanging down from the top of the house, several storeys above her. A large grandfather clock ticked from a recess to her left, and she could smell the faint scent of paint.

Seth observed her. He was fixated by her mouth. He watched her sniffing the air and smiled reassuringly. "I've been doing a lot of interior design around the house. I'll show you later," he said, casually.

Cilla nodded, and he took her arm to lead her through the house to his kitchen. This was a cool room, with everything either white or stainless steel, and immaculately clean. Seth excused himself after asking her to help herself to whatever she wanted and disappeared back the way they had come.

A fresh loaf of bread had been placed in a pristine

bread bin, so Cilla cut half a dozen slices and toasted them. She located the fridge and found the butter, but she couldn't find any Marmite. In fact, she couldn't find anything in the cupboards worth spreading on the toast. The cupboards were beautifully organised but contained little of nutritional value.

The toast popped out of the toaster. Seth had still not returned. Cilla poked her head out of the kitchen door and listened. She could hear music playing somewhere in the house, and the grandfather clock ticked ominously in the hall. Otherwise there was silence. Cilla listened hard and shivered suddenly. Something seemed amiss.

She left the kitchen and moved into the hall. The mellow glow of lamps illuminated the way, and she opened doors as she went, locating a library, a music studio, and a large lounge. She called out for Seth but received no response. She heard the tremble in her voice.

This is ridiculous she thought. He had probably gone up to his bedroom to get changed and fallen asleep. Or perhaps he had decided on a shower. Would she look desperate and stupid if she went up in search of him?

She stood quietly at the bottom of the stairs. Again she could smell paint. It smelt fresher now as though someone in the house had started painting. Cilla checked the time: 2.42 a.m. She supposed Seth might be artistic. Perhaps he painted at night. Rock stars lived odd lives after all. She called again, and when she received no response she started to climb the stairs.

The smell of oil based paint grew ever stronger. Cilla recognised it from her years of working as part of a stage crew. Mostly she painted things a rich oily black. Cilla moved along the first landing from bedroom to bedroom. The furnishings were simple but expensive, with a great deal of cream and beige everywhere, positively dull to

Cilla's eyes.

The master bedroom however had been decorated in black and silver. With relief Cilla heard the shower running in the en suite, and she peeked into the bathroom to see Seth's form outlined beyond the glass.

Smiling, she turned and retraced her steps. Could it be feasible that this amazing rock superstar liked her? A plain and simple stagehand from a small town in the North of England? She hoped he would let her shower too. She had had a long day shifting sound gear and lights, helping out with anyone who needed an extra pair of hands.

The smell of paint seemed stronger here. It appeared to be drifting down from the next landing up. Out of curiosity and feeling more secure, Cilla climbed the stairs to the next floor. This landing was far less opulent. The wood was plain, the floorboards bare. There were large ladders propped against the wall and paint trays and protective cloths scattered around. Several doors opening onto the landing stood ajar. The rooms beyond were empty. Obviously this part of the house had yet to be completed. Cilla lost herself in an adolescent fantasy. She imagined a nursery up here for her babies, but then she caught her breath. What a stupid romantic dream. She knew the reality was more likely to be one night of misspent passion and Seth would not remember her name in the morning.

She turned back to the staircase and started to descend.

A moan from behind her stopped her in her tracks. She stood still and listened.

Nothing.

Cilla frowned. She held her breath and listened. She thought she must have imagined the noise, but then it came again. Yes, no mistaking it.

Cilla moved towards the noise and paused at the door. She held her breath and listened carefully. Another moan. It sounded thick and despairing, like a large animal in pain. With her heart beating hard in her chest, Cilla twisted the handle of the door. It rattled loosely, but it was locked. The moaning intensified on the other side of the door, and Cilla knew she had to get in. She hesitated. She took a few steps back and ran at the door, hitting it side on with her shoulder. The door gave easily, and Cilla almost fell into the room.

Cilla didn't understand what appeared in front of her. It was a large room at the back of the property. The walls were hung with stage blacks; dense heavy material that absorbed light. Dotted strategically around the room were some large stage lights suspended from lighting gantries. They were trained on a sculpture of some kind that inhabited the middle of the room. The sculpture sat on a floor cloth, which had probably once been black, but was now a lustrous shade of powder blue. The sculpture, or carving, or whatever you chose to call it, had been covered completely in light blue paint that shimmered softly in the light. Cilla stared at the sculpture in amazement. Was this an installation? Had Seth bought it? Or had he created it?

The sculpture had been lit with clever use of stage lighting. Shadows flickered across the ceiling. Something in the room, something besides Cilla, had moved. Cilla jumped, startled. Adrenaline coursed through her blood stream. She drew a ragged breath and looked around. Nothing. Just her and the installation.

Cilla inwardly smirked at herself. How ridiculous.

She stared at the sculpture—for what else could she call it—in horrified fascination. At first she thought it had been carved using wood. Solid branches seemed to be sticking out at angles, distorted and reaching. Cilla stood, cocking her head to one side and squinting at what she was looking at. She reconsidered. The branches seemed to be all arms and legs. Those at the bottom of the pile looked like twisted and gnarled tree roots. But those higher up—and the pile stood approximately three to four feet high—did look more like limbs. Yes, in fact, Cilla moved closer … this appeared to be a pile of sculpted bodies, tangled up together.

Cilla stepped towards the sculpture to get a closer look and then pulled herself up short. The moaning noise had come again, and it seemed to be coming from the sculpture in front of her.

Cilla paused and then moved determinedly forwards. Her feet made sticking noises when she walked over the drying paint. She could make out heads and hair, torsos and breasts on the pile. The bodies were stacked up. But this was one amorphous structure, wasn't it? The paint masked any real detail; it could be described as more of a suggestion of a pile of bodies. Isn't that what modern art did? Suggested something to the viewer? Quite clever really.

Cilla felt suddenly doubtful.

She peered more closely at the sculpture, and her heart stopped for one awful second. Suddenly she knew, and her knees turned to water. The figure on the top of the sculpture was alive. It was a naked woman. Cilla could see the rise and fall of her breasts as she struggled to breathe. Her mouth opened and closed like a fish out of water, and paint bubbles blew from her nose. When she moaned, even her mouth and tongue were blue, and Cilla wondered whether someone had poured blue paint down her throat.

Cilla dug her fingers into the paint around the woman's face. The woman cried out in pain and fear. With shaking hands, Cilla clawed at the paint around the woman's eyes and mouth. Underneath Cilla could see a faint hint of pink skin. The hair had congealed and matted and completely stuck to whatever was underneath. With a growing horror, Cilla realised that this was no representation. No. This was an actual pile of human bodies. One artfully arranged on top of another, the paint thrown over each new addition so that they were stuck together forming a single mass.

More frantically now, Cilla tried to free the woman from the pile. Using the sides of her thumbs, she scraped the paint away from her face as best as she could. The woman's eyes were grey, and she watched, terrified, as Cilla tried to free her. "It's okay. It's okay," Cilla chanted, as much to herself as the woman. "I'm going to get you out of here. I'm going to get us both out of here."

Cilla started to work on the hands and arms but realised that the woman had been tied to the bodies beneath her. Shaking, Cilla stared at the bonds in disbelief. She would need something to cut the rope away from her. "I have to get a knife. A knife. Wait. Just a minute. I'll be back. I promise. It's going to be ok." Cilla could hear the quivery panic in her voice, and she cut off a sob and tried to pull herself together. If she was going to rescue the woman and get her out of here, she needed to act fast and decisively.

Turning, she ran straight into Seth's fist.

Her nose exploded in a rush of red, and she fell backwards onto the bodies behind her. She pushed against them and scrambled with her feet, trying to gain purchase on the sticky, wet floor. Seth punched her again on the side of the head, and she crumpled, lying dazed on the floor, while the blood from her nose ran down into her mouth and stars danced in her outer vision.

Seth hauled her to her feet and threw her on top of the pile of bodies next to the moaning woman. Cilla tried valiantly to pull away, but Seth punched her in the stomach and she curled into a ball and then twisted to her side, trying to protect her head with her hands. Seth pulled her arms away one by one and tied them off. He looped a rope around her neck and pulled her head back so that it was trailing off the pile and her long dark hair draped down towards the floor. Seth reached for her legs, and Cilla managed to kick him hard. She heard him curse, but he quickly had her under control. He splayed her legs wide apart and tightened the ropes viciously. When she cried out, he pulled on them again, and Cilla felt the ropes digging deep into her flesh, burning and pinching mercilessly.

He set about cutting her clothes off with a long bone-handled knife. The blade was dull and occasionally he simply ripped the clothes from her, pulling her hard against the rope ties so that she cried out repeatedly.

Seth moved out of Cilla's vision for a while. She could hear him moving around in front of her. Occasionally he sighed, but with her head pulled so far back she couldn't see what he was doing. A draft came from somewhere, probably up the stairs from the hall below. She lay unable to move, naked, cold, and exposed.

Finally Seth appeared in her line of vision just to the side. Twisting her head slightly and straining her eyes to the left she could see that he was naked. He disappeared again and the next minute she could feel him nuzzling between her legs with his flaccid penis. He reached for her nipples, hard and pointed because of the cool temperature of the room. She heard him moan in

133

satisfaction as he pinched both of them. She cried then and begged him to stop. He pinched her breasts hard and dug his nails into her tender skin, leaving welts of blood in crescent shaped holes.

Seth drew away again. For a second Cilla was hopeful that he would finish and disappear, but no. He quickly returned. This time he was clutching a gallon can of powder blue paint and pouring it all over her. He emptied the can, stood back to admire his work and then began to rub the paint into Cilla's skin.

He rubbed and stroked her like a lover, his hands slippery with blue lubricant, firstly taking in her neck and shoulders, caressing her breasts, her stomach and pubis. His fingers were gentle now, tweaking her nipples and then slipping into the folds between her legs. He sighed in satisfaction. He was gentle and attentive and no part of her body went unexplored. More importantly, no part of her body from the shoulders down remained uncovered. He picked up another can and repeated the procedure again. And then again. The paint was starting to dry and harden in places and Cilla tried desperately to keep wriggling and moving, but Seth's peculiar massage was oddly hypnotic and gradually Cilla gave herself up to it.

Seth moved around to her head, and bending down he smiled into her eyes. "You are so beautiful," he said. "You're the cherry on my blue cake."

Seth picked up another can of paint and poured this onto Cilla's hair. He worked it through her thick locks, scrunching and rubbing her hair so that every strand was covered. Cilla's head dangled back, becoming heavier and heavier.

"It's quick drying paint." Seth explained to her. "It's very expensive. I have this colour custom made. Well, I can afford it, can't I?"

Seth started at her face. Cilla closed her eyes tightly and tried desperately to keep her mouth shut, but Seth had other ideas and his intrusive fingers worked their way into her ears, nose and mouth. The taste of paint was bitter in her mouth, making her gag and retch, but Seth was determined. "Don't fuss so, sweetheart. It will be worse for you if you do. You can't sit up now, and you don't want to choke on your own vomit do you? That would be such a rock star way to go. And so messy."

When he was done, Seth moved away and out of her line of sight once more. Cilla heard the door click shut behind him, and she struggled against her bonds. She felt paint sucking and bubbling as she wriggled, but there was no way to free herself. She opened her eyes and opened and closed her mouth to stop the paint solidifying, but it became increasingly difficult. She lay for what seemed like hours, her body becoming more and more immobile. She was completely unable to move her head, her hair felt heavy and solid. Time passed and she found herself praying.

Hours later, Seth came back into the room. He stood in front of Cilla's face, but about eight feet away so that she could see the whole of him in all of his glory. He happily modelled a bright red robe. Freshly shaven, he had obviously cleaned the paint from himself and now smelled fragrant and expensive, with his wet hair framing his face in gentle waves. He dropped the robe off his shoulders so that Cilla could see that he had scrawled 'Rock God' in kohl eyeliner on his hairless chest.

"We're going to have so much fun, you and I, baby," said Seth. "Days and days of it. Then I'm playing four gigs in Germany, but if you're still up for it when I get back we can play again."

Seth dropped his robe completely, and Cilla found

herself eye to eye with his enormous erection. Seth was swollen and wanting, and suddenly Cilla understood what the sculpture was for, why she was lying fixed and immobile in this position, at this angle, with her throat and mouth exposed. She stiffly opened her throat and screamed as loudly as she could as he moved towards her face.

# ACKNOWLEDGMENTS

I've been writing short stories for the past five years –a relative newbie - so some of these tales are early ideas, that formed bigger ideas, and became monsters. Does anyone recognize Aefre from CRONE in 'In Kindness'? I do. I hope you found something among them that was enjoyable.

I owe my writing learning curve to a few key people. To Alex Davis who held a horror weekend in Derbyshire which I attended in November 2012. Alex blew my mind with his wealth of knowledge and I learned a huge amount which set me off with short story writing. Simon Bestwick ran a workshop on the Sunday of that weekend, and the content has stayed with me ever since. I find him inspirational. Thanks to both!

I owe a massive debt of gratitude to Charlie Haynes from The Writer's Playground, because she has facilitated and encouraged my writing every step of the way for five years now.

To my Dad, because he shares his short stories with me and we get competitive!

To John Wycherley, who is never afraid to tell me, "That's rubbish." Only those stories that pass muster with my husband made it into this anthology, so you can thank him for his quality control. Or not ...

And finally, to you, my reader. Thank you for honouring my stories by reading them. It means the world to me. Mind how you go now! X

**Jeannie Wycherley, 21st July 2017**

# ALSO BY JEANNIE WYCHERLEY

*If you go down to the woods today, you'd better not go alone.*

If you enjoyed *Deadly Encounters*, you may like Jeannie's debut novel, **Crone**, released 3rd May 2017.

*"I stood in front of the tree once more, the bark rough beneath my fingertips. This time I knew the truth. I swore on my son's life that he would be avenged. Somehow, someway, I would have my revenge."*

Heather Keynes' teenage son died in a tragic car accident. Or so she thinks. However, deep in the wilds of the Devon countryside, an ancient evil has awoken ... No-one is safe.

When Heather determines the true cause of her son's death, she is hell-bent on vengeance. Determined to halt the march of the Crone once and for all, hatred becomes the ultimate weapon. Furies collide in this twisted tale of murder, magic and salvation.

**Crone** is a mild horror, dark fantasy, part mystery, part thriller, so there's something for everyone, and is available from the usual places.

Jeannie's Autumn 2017 release will be the psychological horror, *The Jumpers*. If you would like further information about this or any new releases, please do sign up for the newsletter
@ http://www.jeanniewycherley.com

You can tweet Jeannie @thecushionlady
Find Jeannie on Facebook: Jeannie Wycherley

# PRAISE FOR CRONE
# BY JEANNIE WYCHERLEY

"Kept me gripped right until the end."

"A real page-turner, atmospheric, with twists and turns and a dizzying climax!"

"Nothing was certain or predictable. A dark and dangerous read
    rooted in a world that's real and recognisable but takes you into truly magical realms."

"One of those stories that taps into natural fears, stories of old and country life. I enjoyed every page of it."

"Stunningly atmospheric! Gothic & timeless set in the beautifully described Devon landscape .... Twists and turns."

"Crone is a really good horror read. For a debut novel, it is impressive."

"I just couldn't put it down particularly at the end. I kept thinking how the hell is Heather going to get out of this crazy situation? The plot was really clever, fantastical but really believable too."

"There was a richness to even the more peripheral and background characters. This was a really impressive debut novel."

"Incredibly twisty and dark but also beautiful and lyrical, this book is one that you won't want to put down.

# ABOUT THE AUTHOR

Jeannie Wycherley is a writer, copywriter and gift shop proprietor who resides somewhere between the forest and the coast in East Devon, UK. Her work is inspired by the landscape, not least because her desk affords her sweeping views over a valley and the glorious hills beyond. Why this translates into horror is anybody's guess.

# PREVIOUSLY PUBLISHED

A Conversation with Death (by Betty Gabriel) was previously published in **Things That go Bump in the Night!** Women in Horror Month, by The Sirens Call eZine, February 2016.

Gretel's Revenge (under the name Betty Gabriel) was published in the horror anthology **Bones II**, edited by James Ward Kirk, (January 2014);

An Encounter with Old Duir was first published in **All women – all horror**, Women in Horror Month, by The Sirens Call eZine, Issue 31, February 2017.

Dog Eared      (produced as Dog Ear and appearing under the name Jeannie Alderdice) first appeared as a podcast, narrated and produced by William Macrae-Smith, with music and sound effects from soundsnap.com. More horror awaits you at **midnightcircle.com**

Make Do and Mend (under the name Betty Gabriel) first appeared in **Body Parts Magazine**, Issue #6: Grave Robbing, June 2016      .

Managing Murder (under the name Betty Gabriel) first appeared in **Slaughter House: The Serial Killer Edition - Volume 1** published by Siren's Call Publications (2013)

Scratching in the Dust (under the name Betty Gabriel) first appeared in **The Lost Door** by Zimbell House Publishing (August 2016).

In Kindness (under the name Betty Gabriel) first appeared in **Off Track: Anthology** from The Writer's Playground (2016).

The Installation (under the name Betty Gabriel) first appeared in **Infernal Ink Magazine** (October 2014).

www.ingramcontent.com/pod-product-compliance
Lightning Source LLC
Chambersburg PA
CBHW020138180626
46810CB00004B/1626